MEMOIRS OF A WANNABE SEX ADDICT

MEMOIRS OF A WANNABE SEX ADDICT

JULIA MORIZAWA

Fanny Press
Seattle, WA

Published by Fanny Press
PO Box 95462
Seattle, WA 98145

Cover design by Sabrina Sun

Contact: info@fannypress.com

ISBN: 978-1-60381-430-0

Contents

The Slave

Scott ran his fingers through my hair and told me I was beautiful. When he said it, he looked me straight in the eyes. He wouldn't look away until I gave him a response. I knew this, so I stared right back. I took in every detail of his eyes so I would never forget the power behind them. The color, a blue so magical, as if the ocean and the sky had blended together after a storm. The shape, deep and wide, like the comforting shelter of a mother's womb. I took in his long, feminine lashes and his perfectly arched brows. I could see his honesty, his passion, and a mysterious history that held years of unrevealed struggle. When my observations caused an intense fluttering sensation in my stomach, I finally turned up the corners of my mouth, ever so slightly, and said, "Thank you."

I often wished that Scott and I were the type of people who could fall in love. The type of people who weren't afraid to do so. But to him, I was just a girl, and he was looking for a woman whom he could marry. And to me, he was just a home away from home. A comfortable set of arms that held me so much tighter than my boyfriend's. And both of us just wanted to hold on because it was a place of stability outside of our everyday hectic and unhappy lives.

My response made him blush. He gently pulled me toward him and kissed me on the forehead. The kind of kiss a father gives to his young daughter at bedtime. Scott was sitting in his thinking chair, an antique coated in burgundy velvet that could have easily belonged in a Charlotte Bronte novel. I'm sure the chair had experienced a lot of skin. A lot of bodily fluids and heavy breathing. That's why I liked it so much. It was a great piece of furniture to have sex on.

I was straddling him and my knees had begun to get sore. I adjusted my body so I was sitting in his lap, my legs dangling over one arm of the chair and my head resting against the other. I pressed my ass hard against his crotch before settling down.

"Where's your boyfriend?" he asked.

"I don't know."

"He sounds like an asshole."

I didn't reply. My boyfriend wasn't an asshole. In fact, no man had ever treated me better than he did. But we bored each other.

I focused my attention on a tall, thin bong centered on his dresser. It was a blood red color with Japanese letters made of silver etched in the side. I didn't know what it said, but probably something about peace or unity. It matched the fresh red paint on the walls. It matched the red silk pillows on his bed. It matched the red beads hanging from the door frame. Everything matched. It was almost suffocating.

"What are you thinking about?" Scott interrupted my silence.

"Nothing," I whispered.

"Don't lie."

I thought about it for a moment. I thought about the red, the suffocation, the way I felt with him.

"Life," I finally concluded.

"What about it?"

"I don't know."

He leaned into me as if he were going to whisper something in my ear. Instead, he kissed the top part of it, then slowly ran the tip of his tongue around the outside, and eventually bit the lobe around my earring. He leaned back. I could feel his stare, could sense he was about to say something else, so I turned to face him.

"I love the way you look when you're thinking hard about something."

Scott and I met at a Fourth of July barbeque. I went to see some acquaintances that I hadn't spoken to in a while. My acquaintances were Scott's closest friends. I immediately went to the bar and he was there pouring drinks for others. He was the type of man who looked best tired and messy. I watched his light curls brush the crease in his forehead every time he looked down. I watched his pink lips purse to the side each time he searched for a specific drink on the table. I was hypnotized by those lips. They looked as if they could never tell a lie. Or never tell a joke. He glanced up and caught me watching him. He offered to pour me a drink.

"What are you having?" I asked.

"Diet Coke," he replied. "I don't drink alcohol."

"Good for you. I could go for a screwdriver."

He smiled, made me the drink, and handed it to me. When our fingers touched in the passing of the glass, the area between my thighs began to throb. We didn't separate from each other the rest of the night. We talked about everything, from the weather, to the party, to our jobs, to politics, to God. We stood on the hillside together to watch the fireworks above the river. Once the show was over, most people left or went back down to the house for more drinks and small talk. We stayed. We lay down on an open patch of grass and shared a joint. We kept a look-out for shooting stars. The lights from the city illuminated the horizon. The shadowed blend and repetition of the trees around us faintly resembled a Warhol installment. Without the shimmering stars, the smooth, black sky could have easily been mistaken for water. Occasionally, the sound of a passing car below us or erupted laughter from the party echoed against the grass. But the sounds of our peaceful, steady breathing kept us oblivious to any disturbances. After a long, beautiful moment of silence, Scott said to me, "It was meant for us to meet here and be together tonight."

When he said that, I couldn't help but turn onto my side and face him. I couldn't help but feel a sudden rush of passion flow through my body. He turned toward me as well and wrapped his arm around my waist. He slowly rubbed his warm hand up and down my back, first over my shirt, then under it. When he kissed me, it was as if all the warmth in his body had been passed over into mine. I wrapped my palm around the back of his neck to pull him in closer, to kiss him harder. His tongue felt like warm silk in my mouth. When he moved it around and under mine, it was done perfectly, as if we had choreographed the movements ahead of time. He caressed my stomach with his hand, making my muscles tense up. When we kissed harder, he grabbed my skin tightly. He slid his hand under my bra and gently cupped my breast, then massaged it, moving it any way he wanted. I kept one hand on his neck and slipped the other underneath his shirt, feeling a thin trail of fuzz just below his naval. I pinched his nipples hard between my fore-finger and thumb. I knew he liked it because of the soft, airy grunts escaping from the back of his throat. He slid his other hand up the back of my skirt and squeezed my thigh, then my ass. I moved my hand from his chest to his stomach to his crotch. I could feel him hard underneath his jeans. After undoing the button and zipper of his pants, I wrapped my fist around his cock, first over his boxers, then under. As I slowly slid my fist from tip to base and back to the tip again, his breathing became heavier, his vocalizations more difficult to control. He followed my lead and pulled my underwear to the side so I could feel a cool breeze pass through my moist skin. He pushed his fingers inside of me, first one, then two, then three. I briefly pulled my hand away to spit in my palm and used it to moisturize his cock. I began to move my wrist and arm faster and he did the same with his fingers. I could feel his pre-cum dripping into my hand, helping me keep him lubricated. Our hips danced with our hands, synchronized in motion together. Suddenly, he pulled himself out of my grasp.

"Stop, stop," he whispered.

"Why, what happened?" I asked.

"Nothing. I just want you to come first."

He sat up, grabbed my ankles and pulled them toward him. He lifted my skirt and slipped my underwear off and let them hang on his wrist. He spread my legs open and held onto the insides of my thighs. I closed my eyes and rested my head against the dry grass. I felt his warm, wet tongue tease my groin, then the lips of my pussy, then my clit. He started slow and gentle. My breathing became heavy and a soft moan escaped my mouth. As he began to pick up speed, he slipped his fingers back inside of me and used his other hand to pinch my nipples. As soon as I came, he reached for his wallet and found a condom. He quickly opened the packaging and slipped the rubber around his hard cock. He leaned into me but stopped and asked, "Is this what you want?" I simply nodded. I watched him penetrate me for the first time. I squeezed myself tight around him and I could tell that he liked it. He felt so good inside of me.

We spent the rest of the night on that hill together. At one point a couple of men walked by. When they spotted us they quickly mumbled an apology and left. By the time the sun was rising, we were alone. Only a few others had crashed at the party, but they were all indoors. From then on, I spent at least three nights a week with him. We never got bored.

"There's so much going on inside of you," he continued, "It only makes me want to know you better."

I smiled and pressed my lips against his. "Do you have to work in the morning?" I asked.

"No, do you?"

"Yes, but I never sleep anyway."

He reached around me to grab his pipe and stash off the window sill. I watched him carefully pack the bowl and take a hit. He gestured for me to come closer. So I did. He wrapped his mouth around mine and exhaled the smoke into my throat. I took it in and slowly released it into the room. I couldn't help but cough a little. I watched the lines around his mouth curl as he took another hit. Sometimes he looked old. Times like these when I could tell he was tired and distracted. I was nineteen at the time. He was twelve years my senior. He still looked young and healthy, but sometimes I could see the age in him sneak to the surface. I caught a glimpse of us in the mirror and we looked beautiful together. I started to suck on his neck, but not too hard, so I wouldn't leave marks. I pushed my tongue inside his ear and rotated it in circles. He groaned. He always loved that.

"Careful," he warned, not meaning it.

"Why?" I tease.

"Because. You'll make me do bad things to you."

"That's what I want."

"I know it is."

I bit his earlobe nice and hard. Hard enough to almost break skin. In retaliation, he grabbed me by the waist, lifted me off of him, and threw me back in the chair. Then he was on top. He ripped off my shirt and my pants and kissed every part of my body. He unclipped my bra and pulled it away so he could suck on my erect nipples. He pushed his fingers inside of me, but only for a moment, just to make sure I was wet. Then he stopped. He stood up and just looked at me for a moment. I smiled. He smiled. We kept our eyes locked tight on each other as he slowly stripped himself naked. He removed his jeans and his cock emerged from within, already hard. He loved not wearing underwear.

He loved letting his pants hang low so the top of his pubic hair was just barely peeking out. He slowly caressed himself, teasing me, letting me watch but not touch. Then he swaggered toward me, back into the chair. This time, he straddled me and pushed in close so the tip of his cock was level with my mouth. He wrapped his hand around my neck, just tight enough to turn me on but not hurt me. I teased him with my tongue. Just barely touching the head then pulling away. Kissing it but not opening my mouth. Licking it but not sucking. He became impatient and tightened his grip around my neck. I smirked then placed one hand around his cock and the other on his ass. I pulled him in closer, letting him slide to the back of my throat. I held him in my mouth for a moment, pursing my lips tight around the base, pushing my tongue hard against the underside. Then finally, I sucked. I sucked hard, using every muscle in my mouth to tickle his nerves. He released his grip around my neck and transferred it to the back of my head, helping me make the complete movements at the desired speed. He let his head fall back, his eyes closed, and he released a moan of complete satisfaction.

We liked to play games with each other. Our favorite was when he played the Master and I was his Slave. He'd call me up in the middle of the night and demand a full-body massage. If I was in the mood, which I often was, I'd make the short drive to his apartment, struggle to find parking, and enter his room at his complete service. When I'd arrive, I'd find him already in bed, lying on his stomach, completely naked. I could see the stiffness in his toned, hairless back. The relaxed muscles in his ass. The blonde hair coating the skin on his legs. I often wanted to climb on top of him right then and there. But I knew I had to be a good girl and be patient, giving him what he had called me over for first. I'd slowly climb on the foot of the bed, lightly dragging my fingernails up the backs of his calves, then his thighs. I'd let one finger gently slip between his ass and tease his hole just for a moment. Then I'd straddle his thighs and get comfortable for the work to come. We kept a bottle of vanilla body oil on the bed stand. I'd grab it and pour a perfect circle of the thick liquid in the palm of my hand. I could feel the coolness travel through my wrist and into my body, creating a tingling sensation that moistened my pussy. Then I'd rub the lotion between my hands, letting the silk sink into my pores. I could hear Scott's breaths become shorter as he grew impatient. I'd use all my weight to dig into the dips just below his shoulder blades and rub the oil from my skin into his. I'd grab his body hard, holding as much as I could get. He was warm and soft, like clean laundry just removed from the dryer. Touching him felt like stepping into a hot tub after a long week of labor and overtime. The vanilla scent would creep into my nostrils, causing a feeling of floatation. I'd move my hands from the back of his neck down to his ass and eventually to his toes. Sometimes the massage would last for as long as half an hour, but usually, he'd want to take it elsewhere after several minutes. He'd flip over, interrupting my work.

"Get off of me! Lay down on the bed," he'd demand.

I'd do as I was told, knowing what would be coming. He kept a line of rope wrapped loosely around one of the bed posts. He'd use it to tie my wrists together above my head and secure me to the bed. I wasn't allowed to talk unless he gave me permission or wanted an answer to a question. I'd have to finish everything I said with, "Master." He always removed my clothing in the same order. My socks, then my pants or skirt, followed by my shirt, which he'd leave dangling around my elbows. He'd slap his cock hard against my body—my legs, my stomach, my face. He'd remove my bra and underwear. Then he'd stand back and just look at me. I could sense him observing the wetness between my legs while he jerked off. Then he'd return to me and rub his pre-cum on my nipples and my clit. He'd tease me, let me lick the tip just so I could get a taste. Then he'd begin pushing the underside of his cock against my clit. Rubbing it, massaging my pussy, but not entering me. He'd ask rhetorical questions or demand details on how much I wanted him.

"Where do you want it?" he'd ask.

"Inside of me, Master."

"What part of you?"

"Anywhere you want to put it, Master."

He'd ask me if he was better than other men. If he had more stamina. If he made me come faster and better. He'd demand I talk dirty to him. He'd demand I describe how I wanted him to fuck me and where. And who would be watching. Eventually, I'd say something that didn't satisfy him.

"That's not what I wanted to fucking hear!" he'd scream. Then he'd flip me over, my wrists still attached to the bed post. He'd grab me by the waist and force me onto my knees. He'd pull his arm back and slap my ass. He'd slap me so hard I could feel the heat soar up into my arms. And he wouldn't stop until I apologized. I'd hold out until the pain was too much to take.

"I'm sorry, Master," I'd cry out. "Please forgive me, I'll do whatever you want, Master."

"Do you promise?"

"I promise, Master."

He'd stop the hits, but keep his hands tight around my ass, pulling my cheeks wide apart.

"I believe you," he'd respond. "But this will teach you to be more careful next time."

Then I could feel the head of his cock massage my asshole. He'd lubricate it first with the juices from my pussy. Then he'd slowly push inside. I'd squeeze my ass tight around it until he'd groan. Then he'd push in further, and further, and further. Until he was completely inside of me. He'd get comfortable with the motions before picking up pace. I could feel a tight, sudden pain when he'd push in too far. As his hips moved faster, I could feel his balls slapping against my ass. I braced myself against the pillow, pushing my head against the back board of the bed, grasping tightly to the rope around my wrists. Sweat would begin dripping into my eyes. My hair would cling to my neck. As he'd become rougher, I truly felt like he owned me. I truly wanted him to do anything to me. To abuse me. To use me. To hurt me. My grunts and groans would become louder and faster as the pain became harder to bear.

"Are you going to be more careful next time?" he'd ask through short breaths and erotic grunts of his own.

"Yes, Master," would barely escape from my lips.

"What was that?"

"Yes, Master," I'd repeat a little louder.

"I can't hear you."

"Yes, Master!"

"I still can't hear you!"

"Yes! I promise to be more careful next time, Master." Then I'd begin begging. "Please believe me, Master! Please, I beg you, please believe me!"

When my cries and pleads finally became forceful enough and honest enough for his satisfaction, he'd lean forward on top of me. He'd squeeze my tits with one hand and finger my clit with the other. Then he'd press his face against my neck, his chest against my back. I could feel his heart pounding. It beat in-sync with mine. We would become one in those moments. In those moments of undeniable passion and intensity. Sometimes he would come inside of me, inside of my ass. Other times, he'd pull out at the last minute and come on my lower back. Sometimes it would spray on my neck and into my hair. When he'd finish, he'd massage his cum into my skin with his hand or cock. Then he'd lay on top of me, holding me, our breathing as one. Our bodies as one. Our spirits as one.

Scott pulled himself out of my mouth and slid his cock down my body, from my chin to my thighs. He left a thin trail of liquid on my chest, which quickly became cool once it touched the air. I was still leaning back in the chair, comfortable and secure. He gently parted my legs. I rested my heels on the edge of the cushion, knees bent, so my pussy was wide open to him. He gently massaged the insides of my thighs, then moved to my groin, then to the tiny hairs that had began growing again on my bikini line. I felt a swarm of butterflies emerge in my stomach as he leaned in to kiss my naval. I felt energy flowing from the tips of my fingers and toes as he began to circle my clit with his thumb. My pussy tightened and I was about to lean my head back and close my eyes when I caught him staring at me. The look on his face was completely subdued, honest and reflective. Neither of us said anything. I analyzed the shape of his jaw. His chin, which was perfectly smooth but pink from a recent shave. And his lips. The lips that I could not help but be attracted to since the first time I saw them.

"I love you," he whispered.

I couldn't help but laugh. Soft, but unexpected and rude.

"No, I mean it," he retaliated, "I really love you."

I smiled. He leaned in for a quick kiss. A peck, the kind a boyfriend gives his girlfriend when they're surrounded by family. Then he removed his thumb and replaced it with his warm tongue. He played with my clit, just barely touching it. Then wrapped his lips around it, sucking, kissing, nibbling. I could feel my wetness dripping onto the chair as he began to work faster. The gentle tickle created a magnificent warmth through my body. After only a few minutes, I knew I could come, but prevented myself from doing so because I didn't want him to stop. He knew how I liked it. He knew the best places, the best technique. He knew the right speed and the right pressure. He knew how to make me want to fuck him.

"Scott," I mumbled through heavy breaths, "I want you inside me."

I could hear him fumbling for a condom while he continued going down on me. I could hear him tear the wrapper with one hand and unroll it onto his cock. I could hear him moan as he pushed inside of me. My wetness lubricated his cock more than the condom. It allowed him to move inside of me smoothly, efficiently, perfectly. I pressed the heel of my left foot hard into his ass. I used the toes of my right foot to grip the skin on his side. He reached for my ankles and swung my legs over his shoulders. He never ceased the grinding of his hips. I lifted my head so I could watch us. So I could watch him fuck me. It was beautiful. He flipped me over, slowly so he wouldn't exit my body while doing so. He bent me over the back of the chair and climbed onto it behind me. He continued thrusting and grinding. I had to brace myself against the wall. This was always my favorite position because it allowed him to enter me completely. Because I couldn't see his face and his emotions remained a mystery to me. He fucked me harder and faster so my head repeatedly bumped into the wall. The chair against my stomach was making it more difficult to breathe. My knees began to burn and my thighs began to cramp. His grunts and gasps told me he was about to come. I waited, wondering where he would do it. Would he come into the condom and remain inside of me even after he finished? Or would he quickly pull out, rip the condom off, and come on my back? That night, I was hoping he would do the latter. But instead, he slowed down. He stopped. He pulled out. I turned my head to him.

"Did you come?" I asked.

He shook his head. Then he scooped me up in his arms and stood, holding me tightly. He carried me to the bed, as if we were newlyweds entering the hotel room we had reserved for the first night of our honeymoon. He gently laid me down on the fresh sheets. I could smell the spring scent of detergent on the pillow cases. The sheets felt cool under my body. Soft and clean, like grass after the morning dew has evaporated but the sun hasn't yet emerged. I kept my legs spread, ready to continue. Scott re-entered my body. He lied on top of me, but held himself up so I wouldn't be uncomfortable. He kissed my forehead, my cheeks, my chin, then eventually my lips. Even as his hips fell back into the repetitive motions of sex, he continued kissing me. We never kissed during sex. We'd bite, lick and suck, but never kiss. He didn't pick up speed the way he normally did either. He didn't push himself all the way in. He just continued at this comfortable, gentle pace. Then he held my hand. He locked his fingers between mine. Our sweaty palms clung together. Suddenly, I felt like I was his girl. And he was my man. A tight, threatening knot developed in the pit of my stomach. I felt like the wind had been knocked out of me. It became difficult to breathe, as if I were trapped in a Manhattan subway station on a humid August afternoon. I became light headed and the sounds of us, of the room, started to echo. I felt like I was drowning. Suddenly, I realized what it was. In that moment, Scott was not fucking me. He was not having sex with me. He was making love to me.

Scott and I never once went on a date. We never went out together in public. We were a secret. A private, passionate combination of loneliness and erotic desires. But he was more than a fuck-buddy. He was a good friend. We had conversations that I had only dreamed of starting with my boyfriend, but knew I couldn't. We could spend hours together in complete silence, just holding each other, and that was fine. And the sex was amazing. Physically, he satisfied me completely. He gave me what my boyfriend didn't. He made me feel beautiful.

In that moment, I felt like I loved him. I felt like I could love him forever. I wanted to run away with him and spend the rest of my life in his arms. And I suddenly believed him. I believed that he loved me. I believed that he loved me for who I was, not just for my tits and ass. I no longer felt like a possession, a piece of meat. I felt like his body inside of mine was a true connection, not just an orgasm. And this sudden realization sent a thousand knives through me. My eyes began to water and I allowed tears to slide down the side of my face onto the pillow beneath me. I was confused. I was uncomfortable. And for the first time ever, I wanted him to stop.

For a brief moment, Scott pulled his lips away from mine and lifted his head to get some air. And with a complete lack of control, I pulled my hand away from his and slapped him hard across the face. He stopped, shocked, still inside of me. A look of utter confusion in his eyes. He couldn't tell if I was just playing or not.

"What was that for?" he asked.

"You're being too gentle . . . Master."

"Maybe that's how I want it right now." His voice was serious. Not pretend-serious, not sexy-serious. But downright, honest-to-God serious.

"Bullshit," I challenged. Then I slapped him again. Harder. Time stopped. I saw an infinite number of thoughts and feelings pass behind his eyes. Hurt, fear, confusion, disbelief, love, hate, passion, lust. Then anger. With a sudden force that I had never experienced before, he wrapped one hand tight around my neck and used the other to cover my mouth. He pressed down on me with the full weight of his body and pinned my thighs open with his knees. Then he fucked me. He fucked me so hard it felt like a metal baseball bat was breaking me from the inside out. He fucked me so fast that I could no longer feel the motions. All I could feel was my insides being torn, my organs being smashed, the skin lining my pussy ripping from rawness. Keeping one hand over my mouth at all times, he grabbed the hair on the top of my head and yanked so my chin hit my chest. Then he threw me back into the headboard. He leaned in to bite my neck. The pain from his teeth was unbearable.

It shot through me, paralyzing, almost knocking me unconscious. I tried to pull away but had no strength compared to his. When he leaned back again, I saw a small drop of blood on his bottom lip. I knew it was mine. Every time he banged into me, an unfamiliar and torturous cramp swallowed every nerve in my body. Never ceasing the thrusts of his hips, he let go of my hair and slapped me hard across the face. Then again, only harder. So hard that I felt a sudden pain in my eye and I realized he had knocked my contact lens out of its proper place. He was giving me what I gave him. Letting me know how it felt. Then he grabbed my neck again. My mouth was still covered, but he adjusted the positioning of his hand so it blocked my nasal passages as well. I couldn't breathe. That's all I could think about in that moment. I was not receiving any air. My lungs were swelling. I was crying. I was bleeding. I was bruising. I felt myself scream, but no sound escaped my throat. I thought I was going to die.

"Is this better?" he growled.

I couldn't respond. I had no way to.

"Is it!"

I blinked my eyes rapidly, as a substitution for the nod I couldn't give. My lungs were begging for the air they were no longer receiving. Blood was frantically pumping into my brain.

"Now listen to me closely." He instructed in a low, threatening tone. "I'm going to come. And when I do, I'm going to release my hands, and you're going to tell me that you love me. Do you understand?"

I blinked again. He continued ramming into me, merciless. Then his voice turned into loud moans of pleasure and excitement. His muscles tensed, his jaw clenched, as his fluids begged to be released. He quickly removed his hands from my neck and mouth and placed them on my breasts, squeezing them both rough in his fists.

"Tell me that you love me," he demanded through his orgasmic moans.

"I love you," my voice was barely audible, not even a whisper.

"Louder!"

"I love you."

"Say it again!"

"I love you!"

"Say it again!"

"I love you!" I cried out in desperation, tears streaking down my face, praying to a God I didn't believe in to make him stop.

And he finished. He collapsed but stayed inside of me. Our bodies pulsated from the event, throbbing around each other. He cradled my head in his arms and pressed it against his own. He buried his face between the sheets and my ear. He saw my tears and gently wiped them away with his fingers. He held me like I was his child.

"I'm sorry," he whispered into my ear.

I wanted to say "Don't be," or "It's okay," but I remained silent.

"You bring out the worst in me," he continued.

I felt his warm body against mine. His gentle hands caressing my skin. His honesty. His pain. His love.

"I know," I answered, "I know."

I didn't hear from him for a week. I expected that though. I wanted to give him some time. I wanted to give myself some time. I had spent that week contemplating the experience. Wondering why I preferred for him to hurt and violate me than to hold and love me. Why it felt so wrong for a man to be gentle. Why I couldn't get turned on unless it was rough. I didn't see my boyfriend at all during that week either because the bruises on my neck and between my thighs needed time to fade away. I wanted to avoid an interrogation. So I could avoid telling the truth.

Scott finally called me on a Thursday at about three in the morning.

"Hey, baby," he always began our phone conversations the same way.

"Hey," I replied.

"Did I wake you?"

"No, I was just getting ready for bed."

After some general small talk and the sharing of our past week, he said, "We can't do this anymore."

"I know."

And I did. I understood. I agreed. I had come to the realization that two negatives don't make a positive. That it was a bad idea to have two fucked up people taking their issues out on one another in bed.

"You don't know the power you have over me," he stated. Honest. Sincere.

The silence over the phone was long. But not uncomfortable. That's how it was with us. Finally, I told him the truth.

"I love you."

"I love you, too."

Silence again. Neither of us wanted to hang up. We kept assuming the other would have the balls to do it first. And he was the one that did.

"Good night," he said.

"Good night."

I waited to hear the click on his end. Even then, I didn't remove the phone from my ear until the dial tone began to beep.

The Disciple

The earth was not created in seven days. It was created in eight. And on the eighth day, God said, "Let there be a man whom my daughter, Eve, shall desperately desire, and my son, Adam, shall viciously envy for all eternity." And then there was him. And God named him Lucas, and allowed him to travel the lands alone. If biblical history had been written correctly, the eighth day of the week would have been named after Lucas. But the people decided that because of his seductive power, the use of his name could not be allowed. In my new testament, Lucas was not the abandoned son of God. He was God.

We called him Angel Eyes because he had the most hypnotic, ocean blue eyes ever created. I caught myself starting into them and felt as if some infinite power had lifted all the weight off my shoulders and replaced it with two gentle hands and half a bottle of cocoa butter. When he shifted his eyes and noticed me, I immediately turned away, feeling as if I had been caught taking a bite out of the apple. I thought about approaching him, but held back in fear of committing too many sins in a single evening. Instead, he approached me.

It was the first day. The bar was crowded because of karaoke night. Each pool table contained a dozen stacks of quarters reserving spots to play the winner. The men were still dirty after a long day of tarring roofs and tiling floors.

The women were lotioned and bare-legged in a battle to take the best-looking or wealthiest man home. Both wealth and looks were always minimal at the bar, but Lucas was by far at the top of the list for the latter.

He introduced himself and asked my name. I told him, consciously biting my full bottom lip. I leaned my chin down, lifted my eyes up, and smiled. He smiled back, but didn't break his stare. He placed a drink token on the table in front of me then excused himself for a cigarette. I gave it about thirty seconds before I followed him out the back door. He stood patiently, as if waiting for me. He offered me a light and we silently smoked together. The parking lot was brighter than the interior of the bar, so I was able to examine his full frame. He was beautifully built. His arms were covered with intricate tattoos. I could make out several more on his chest through his thin, white wife-beater. His hairline had started to recede, but he wore it well with a smoothly shaved head. He lifted his shirt to show me a small tattoo across his heart. It was his last name, spelled out in beautiful cursive. He told me his brother had the same tattoo. They got them done together when they had begun speaking again.

The conversation ceased as our cigarettes burned out. After another moment of silence, Lucas asked me if I wanted to go to his car for a bump. At the time, I didn't know what he meant by "a bump," but I agreed anyway. We sat in the front of his car while Aerosmith blared on the radio. He pulled a small knife out his pocket and poured two tiny piles of white powder on the edge of the blade. He told me he'd hold the knife for me because he didn't want me to accidentally cut my pretty face. I snorted both piles quickly and almost immediately felt the high. I had never done cocaine before. Lucas reloaded the knife and joined me in euphoria. The alcohol in my body quickly stirred the powder and I suddenly felt amazingly good. I nuzzled my face against Lucas' neck and slowly licked his ear. I quickly pulled away, embarrassed, and giggled. He smiled. Then we exited the car and returned to our drinks.

For the rest of the night I followed Lucas around like a puppy dog. He didn't seem to mind and began introducing me to his friends. I was a newcomer to the bar, but apparently he was a long-time regular. We shot pool, played darts, did just about everything except karaoke. Neither of us considered ourselves singers. Two-o-clock came quickly, and as the bar closed up, he walked me to my car. He opened the door for me, but I was hesitant to get in. Instead, I stood on my toes so I could hug him. As I pulled him in close, I inhaled deeply. He smelled of the country air after a warm, spring shower. I couldn't help but lean in and gently kiss his neck. He placed his palm on my cheek and guided my face until our lips connected. He tasted bitter—a mixture of whiskey and Marlboro lights. But I didn't mind. The warmth of his mouth against mine made me shiver euphorically.

We pulled away from each other when another bar patron shouted some drunk, immature comment at us and ran away laughing. I sat in the driver's seat of my car after Lucas made sure I was okay to drive. When I was finally able to assure him that I was, he said good night and softly shut the door.

The second day came a week later. The karaoke was already in full-throttle when I stepped into the bar. I anxiously looked around for Lucas, but he was nowhere to be found. Instead, there was Clint. He was sitting at the bar alone, sipping on a Miller Genuine Draft. His dark hair was styled to look messy. He was wearing shorts and a baggy sweatshirt with some sort of skateboarding logo on the front. The part of his left leg remaining exposed contained a tattoo of a large, green lizard. I wondered what it represented. I approached the bar and ordered my usual Bacardi and Coke. As I tipped the bartender, Clint turned to me and smiled.

We met in the parking lot a couple of hours later. I was drunk and disappointed that Lucas had never made an appearance. I walked Clint to his truck and sat in the passenger's seat to keep him company while he sobered up for the long trek home. We talked about our exes, our friends and our bar buddies. We talked about our family problems, our work problems and our drinking problems. He gently touched my leg as he told me how much his girlfriend hated him going to the bar. I turned to him and looked him up and down. Without hesitation, I climbed into the driver's seat and straddled him. I ran my fingers through his hair and caressed his cheek. Then I kissed him. I imagined he was Lucas and remembered our mouths dancing together the week before. I teased Clint's tongue with mine and gently pinched his nipples. He did the same to me then grabbed my ass. I slid one hand down his stomach, first over his sweatshirt then underneath it. He pulled off my shirt and lifted my bra so it hung just below my neck. He sucked on my nipples, pinching and squeezing my breasts. I adjusted the positioning of my crotch against his to stop the tingling between my legs. But it only got worse. I cupped my hand around him and felt his hardness through his shorts. I pulled down the zipper and slipped my hand inside his boxers. His cock felt warm and sticky around my fingers. I slowly began to jerk him off as his hips moved in sync with my motions. Once I had helped him grow to his full potential, I slipped off his lap and kneeled back in the passenger's seat. I took off my bra and pulled his shorts and boxers down to his knees. His cock filled my mouth, plus some. I sucked hard, tasting his sweet and salty pre-cum. I fluttered my tongue against the underside of the head. Then I sucked some more, allowing a gentle hum to develop at the back of my throat at the same time. He grabbed my ass harder then lifted my skirt and slipped his hand beneath my panties. He teased my clit and aggressively inserted his fingers inside of me. I moaned, which must have increased the sensation he felt around his cock because he moaned too. He asked me if I had a condom. I told him that I did and quickly reach for my purse and found one. I greedily unwrapped it and unrolled it around his dick. I removed my underwear, lifted my skirt, and sat on top of him. As he entered me, we both moaned again. He sucked on my breasts and spanked me while I bounced up and down on top of him. The windows of his truck had completely steamed up so no one could see us inside. Of course anyone who saw the windows from outside could assume what was going on. When he came, I let him remain inside of me while we both caught our breaths. Before we were able to completely detach ourselves from one another, there was a hard knock on the passenger side window. I couldn't see who it was because the glass was still clouded, but I recognized the voice. It was Chloe, my maternal co-worker who had introduced me the bar. She sounded angry and demanded that I get back inside. She didn't say anything else, but the tone in her voice indicated that I was in trouble.

Clint and I kissed one last time, then he said he should get going anyway. His girlfriend hated him staying out late and had assigned him a regular curfew. I nodded and quickly redressed myself. I suddenly felt like a teenager who had been told she was a beautiful woman by a man who now stated she was a cute little girl. I shook it off by applying lip gloss, grabbing my purse and stumbling out of the truck. Before I was halfway back to the bar, he had pulled away and exited the parking lot.

When I stepped back inside, I teetered in the doorway for a moment to allow my eyes to adjust to the dark flurry of color and movement. There were nearly twice as many people as I remembered and I wondered how long I had been away for. Then on the opposite side of the room, bending over a pool table with cue stick in hand, I saw Lucas. The pocket he was aiming for must have been aligned with where I was standing. He caught a glimpse of me, threw his cue stick on the table, and marched out the other door. My instinct was to follow him, but Chloe appeared out of the shadows and stepped in front of me. She told me to stay away from him. Apparently he had stated publicly that he didn't want sloppy seconds.

As a result of too much liquor or from not taking my meds—or both—I felt the inside of my nose burn as I struggled to choke back tears. I escaped to the bathroom but remained standing at the sink because the one stall was occupied. I sobbed silently, feeling like a failure, a slut, an ass. I felt my cheeks flush and dampen as I grew too warm, then too cold, then too warm again. I hesitated to splash water on my face as it would wash away my already smeared make-up. Instead, I wet a rough paper towel and dabbed my eyes and nose with it.

I heard the stall door unlock then open. A tall, thin woman emerged. She must have been in her early forties. Her hair was bleached a youthful blonde, but her dull roots were in need of a touch up. She sported thigh-tight denim jeans, teal open-toed heels, and a matching halter top that hung a little too low in front. For the most part she was relatively attractive, but regular heavy drinking and partying at a late age was evident in the lines on her face. She was blatantly far gone and the mother in her escaped through over-exaggerated gestures and a high-pitched tone in her voice when she saw me crying. She asked me what was wrong and said I could tell her anything. But first she retrieved a small metal compact from her purse and opened it to reveal a mound of cocaine. She scooped some of the white power into her long, fake pinky nail and held it up to my nose. I obediently plugged my left nostril with my knuckle and snorted up my right. Then she collected another serving, which I also devoured. I felt a sense of relief from the instant high and told her everything that had happened that night so far. Then I backtracked and told her how I had met Lucas just last week and how I was really into him, but that I had quickly screwed things up by fucking Clint just a short while ago. She leaned her back against the wall, bending her knees so she was closer to my height. She did her best to calm me, stroking my head and telling me everything would be fine. She knew Lucas and considered him a close friend. She said she would speak with him on my behalf.

The woman left me alone in the bathroom with half of her cocaine, which I had wrapped up in a dollar bill. I spent the next hour or two between a seat at the bar next to Chloe and locked in the restroom stall sneaking little bumps. Lucas had disappeared.

The third day arrived several hours later, after the bar had long closed for the night. The woman in the restroom had approached Lucas on my behalf and told him that I felt really guilty about what I had done. She had also expressed my attraction to him and explained how I wanted to get to know him on a deeper level. In shorter words, she apologized to him for me. I had been lingering around, mostly chatting with Chloe and chain smoking outside. The woman emerged from the bar and found me in the parking lot. She told me that everything was taken care of. Then she left. A moment later, Lucas appeared and declared that he had reacted unfairly since we barely knew each other and we were not in any sort of relationship. So he invited me to hang out with him and some of his friends.

We spent the night in a two story apartment, snorting lines, playing Uno, and jamming on the owner's sound mixer. Chloe was the only other woman there. Then there were three boys, all friends of Lucas' from the bar, perhaps in their mid-twenties. Everyone was high in a good way. I sat on Lucas' lap while the group discussed everything from music to exes to philosophy. We laughed constantly, but about what exactly, none of us could say. And as each plate of cocaine was snorted away, it was soon replaced with another. I massaged the back of Lucas' neck and admirably watched him converse with his friends. He was obviously the center of the group. Everyone knew each other through him and they all spoke highly of him. Even though I wasn't clear on how he felt about me, in that moment, I felt like his girl. And I felt like the dorky freshman who had won over the senior prom king.

Once the crowd began to die down, Lucas and I snuck off to the upstairs bedroom. The room wasn't totally private because the fourth wall was merely a railing that remained open to the rest of the apartment. So if I peered over, I could see everyone in the living room below. It appeared to serve as a guest room and storage space, and was currently unoccupied.

Lucas and I slipped under a pine green feather comforter on the bed. We laid on our backs, staring up at the ceiling, whispering our conversation to one another. We mostly small-talked about what we did in the daytime. He had recently been fired from his normal nine-to-five job. He sold and installed fancy, decorative aquariums in rich people's homes and corporate offices. He had primarily worked on a commission basis, but had enjoyed the job because it was relatively simple and the money was good. Plus, he got to see inside the types of homes he someday aspired to own himself. But a client had accused him of stealing a large amount of cash from inside his house. Lucas didn't say whether or not he was actually guilty, but the company had no choice but to fire him. He was conflicted because he had little faith he could obtain another job. And dealing drugs had always been a side source of income. He didn't want to do it for a living, but he feared that he had no other choice.

We could hear occasional bursts of laughter from downstairs, but the music drowned out any additional sounds. It was easy to forget that Lucas and I weren't entirely alone. I touched him. I kissed him. He remained on his back and was mostly unresponsive. Not in a way that hinted he wasn't interested, but rather because he didn't want to risk making the wrong move. Or perhaps he simply wasn't the intimate type. I climbed on top of him, straddling his hips. I held his round face in my hands and pressed my lips hard against his. Everything I did, he did back, but I had to do it first. When I opened my mouth, he opened his. When I pressed my tongue against his, he pressed back. When I slipped my hand beneath his shirt, he slipped his under mine. Between my legs, I felt his cock harden under the zipper of his jeans. I leaned my weight back and slowly began to rock against it, allowing the hardness to massage my clit through our layers of clothing. I moved my hand from his chest to his crotch and grabbed him, locating the base and finding the tip. I repositioned myself from my knees to my ass and sat back on the bed so I could unbuckle his belt. His arms released me and rested motionless at his sides. He kept his eyes closed, never looking at me, but never protesting. So I unzipped his pants and pulled them down to his ankles. His erection caused his loose-fitting boxers to hang like a tent half a foot above his thighs. When I pulled his underwear down to lay with his jeans, his cock bounced from the pressure of the elastic then repositioned itself with its head pointing toward Lucas' chest. I removed my own jeans and panties when Lucas' hands remained still and his eyes never fluttered open. Then I climbed back on top of him, straddling his hips again, sandwiching his cock between my legs. I rocked back and forth. The wetness of my pussy instantly lubricated the full length of his penis. I could hear the sounds of wet skin rubbing against wet skin. A quiet moan escaped his lips and I took it as my cue to continue. So I leaned forward until I felt the tip of his cock against my opening. When I rocked back again, I allowed him to slide inside of me. I felt my pussy swallow him whole, without a hint of protest. My body felt a total sense of satisfaction as if I had just officially claimed Lucas as my territory. As his skin rubbed against each centimeter of the tissue within me, bolts of energy shot through every part of my body, creating an entirely new sensation with every charge. Lucas remained unnaturally still, but it didn't bother me because I had no urge for him to pleasure me. I only wanted to pleasure him.

I fell into a rhythm—using the muscles in my thighs to slide my pussy up and down his cock. I braced myself with my arms, my hands on the pillow on either side of his head. Then I closed my eyes too, and centered my focus on the way he felt inside of me. He felt warm and safe. He felt like he could take care of me and I could take care of him. As my legs began to cramp, I realized that the natural sensation of sex had been somewhat numbed by the drugs and alcohol still flowing through my system. After a while, I could no longer tell if he was actually still inside of me. But I assumed he was as his breathing became heavier and his hips gyrated faster against mine. Then he released a single long, low groan, flexed every muscle in his body, then collapsed, limp on the bed. When he stopped, I stopped. Finally, he opened his eyes and stared blankly just past me. I pulled back and found that my pussy had regained its senses as I felt him slide out of me. A cascade of his warm semen flushed out of me and ran down my thighs. I retreated to the bathroom to rinse him off of me. I returned with a large wad of toilet paper so he could do the same. In silence, we redressed ourselves. Then he retrieved a bag of white powder from his wallet and used a nearby CD case to cut us some lines. We swiftly inhaled them and impatiently waited for the short-term pick-me-up. He planted a warm kiss on my cheek and told me I was an amazing person. Then we made our way back downstairs to rejoin the party.

The fourth day occurred a couple of weeks later. Lucas and I had been meeting up nearly every night—sometimes for a few hours at the bar and sometimes until the next morning, bouncing around various apartments and motel rooms. It was a Wednesday night and I had anxiously sped from work directly to the bar. When I arrived, there were only a couple of people sitting by the televisions, none of whom I recognized. I figured most people were still finishing up at work or on their way over. So I ordered myself a Long Island iced tea. I wanted to get drunk as quickly as possible without consuming so much liquid that I would have to pee every five minutes. Plus, although I had grown friendly with most of the regulars at the bar, I still found that I needed to be fucked up to become the sexy, charismatic and fun woman that I had spent my whole life trying to be. I wanted to become that woman before Lucas arrived.

I sat on a tattered wooden bench outside the back door and lit up a cigarette. I watched a ratty red pick-up pull into the parking lot. Two guys emerged from it and I recognized one of them as Casey, the tenant of the two-story apartment where Lucas and I first had sex. I had socialized with him several times since then at the bar and had always found him entertaining. He was in his mid-twenties, arms decorated with tattoos, a dark goatee masking his youthful appearance. The other person I had never seen before. He was around the same age, but he carried himself differently. He seemed to be more of the quiet, artsy type while Casey was the loud, jokester. They approached me together, both flirty and providing me with the attention I so often yearned for. The other guy introduced himself as Ryan. He was from San Francisco and had just moved down to Los Angeles. He was a musician and thought he'd give Hollywood a try. He was staying in the upstairs guest room of Casey's apartment.

The three of us hit it off immediately and as the liquor warmed my body, I found myself extremely attracted to both of them. It wasn't purely sexual, but also the excitement of feeling liked and approved of. They made me feel popular. We talked a lot about music—our favorite bands, albums and songs. We took turns shooting pool and selecting songs in the jukebox. They bought me drink after drink and never let me go outside to smoke alone. Then all of a sudden, it was ten 'o'clock. I realized that Lucas had still not made an appearance and I began to worry. I wasn't worried about his safety, but about the disappointment I would have to endure if I didn't get to see him that night. I shared my concern with Casey, who stated that Lucas was due to stop by his place to bring them some blow. He invited me to join them, so the three of us crammed into his truck and drove the eight blocks to his apartment. When we arrived, Ryan serenaded me on his guitar. He played songs by some of my favorite bands, which we had discussed earlier. Then he played some of his original work, which I was immediately blown away by. Soon, Casey joined him, and the two of them jammed together. I couldn't recall what their music sounded like five minutes later, but I remembered that it was beautiful and in that moment I believed that everything was going to be okay.

Eventually, they were interrupted by a knock on the door. Casey answered it and Lucas entered. He looked exhausted and anxious. He greeted me shortly and planted himself on the couch. He said he couldn't stay long because he had to make some rounds. When I asked if I could trail along with him, he promptly shook his head. He traded Casey an 8-ball for some cash. Casey poured some of the contents of the bag onto a small tile of plexi-glass, which he had obtained long ago solely for this purpose. As a normal form of etiquette, he divvied up some lines and offered them first to Lucas, who quickly snorted two, then passed the dish to me. Keeping to the routine, I inhaled the two largest remaining lines then passed them on to Ryan. And the circle continued. The boys chatted casually while I kept silent and still, only moving when more drugs were hashed out and it was my turn to take them. Within twenty minutes, Lucas excused himself and left the way he came. He wouldn't return that night.

The cocaine lasted us maybe another hour or two. When we ran out, I hastily shelled out the cash to get some more. But it wasn't Lucas who delivered the next batch. It was someone else who came and went fast enough that I never caught his name. By two in the morning, we had lost all ability to maintain logic and sense. It became impossible to stay high without continuously snorting fresh lines and I became anxious for a change of pace. I suggested that we watch some porn. The boys found my proposal amusing and hastily agreed. Casey retrieved a DVD, which opened with two young girls sun-bathing in bikinis next to a pool. Soon enough, they were both naked, trading spit, sucking on each other's tits and eating each other out. The three of us sat on the couch, me sandwiched in the middle. We kept the drugs in easy reach before us, no longer politely taking turns, but rather consuming as much as we wanted as we pleased. I proposed we all get naked, just like the girls in the video, and ungracefully removed my clothing. When the boys did not follow my lead immediately, I climbed on top of Casey, straddling his lap, and aggressively began to grind against his crotch. I pulled his shirt over his head and bit his ear, then his neck, then his shoulder. Eventually, he responded by grabbing my waist and leaning forward in order to take my nipples into his mouth. His goatee felt scratchy and tickled my breasts in a pleasurable way. When I let my head fall back, I saw that Ryan had removed his own shirt and was right up against me. Instinctually, I wrapped my arm around his neck and pulled him in close so I could suck on his chin. While Casey continued sucking and biting one of my nipples, Ryan pinched the other between his fingers. I felt a distinct difference between the sensations experienced by each breast and found that my body's focus was split in two directions. I became overwhelmed by the heightened pleasure and ceased the work of my hands and mouth and hips on them so they could simply service me. I allowed my body to mostly go limp, only moving to accept their actions. Ryan pulled me backwards and guided me onto the couch until I lay across it flat on my back. My ass remained on Casey's lap, except my crotch was then exposed to the air. I threw one leg over Casey's shoulder and onto the back of the couch. I let the foot of my other rest on the carpet below. I realized that, despite the cocaine flowing through my system, my pussy had become moist when a breeze hit it and sent a chill up my back. Ryan knelt on the floor parallel to my chest and leaned over me to alternate the quick flutter of his tongue between my nipples. He squeezed both my breasts tightly in his hands to force them closer together. His licking became sucking. His sucking became biting. I closed my eyes and arched my back, wanting to make myself as open and vulnerable as physically possible. Then I felt something slide into my wet pussy. It was a finger, undoubtedly Casey's. He started off slow, allowing me to experience the different sensations from nail to knuckle and everything in between. He massaged my wetness into my clit before pushing back inside of me, this time with two fingers, then finally, three. When I moaned, he banged me harder and faster. Soon, I no longer felt the movement of his hand but only the tips of his fingers hitting the tunnel walls within me and his knuckles slamming against my pelvic bone.

As my body convulsed from Casey's aggressive intrusions, Ryan pulled away from me and rose. My breasts felt chilly as the air brushed against the saliva he had left on my skin. I titled my head slightly to watch him removed his jeans and underwear in a single fluid motion. His erect cock stared directly at me. Then he stepped up to me again and straddled his legs so his crotch was perfectly level with my face. Without hesitation, I opened my mouth and inhaled his hardness until it hit the back of my throat. It filled my mouth, forcing my saliva to seep onto my lips. The ribbed, pulsating veins of his cock rubbed against my tongue and occasionally bounced against my teeth. I strained to move my head back and forth, massaging every inch. My eyes began to water as I struggled to breathe through my clogged nostrils. My neck tightened and cramped. But I refused to slow down. I wanted to impress him. Ryan must have sensed my struggled because he soon supported the back of my head with one hand and assisted me. I pressed my tongue hard against the underside of his cock, sometimes curling it to slide it into the small slit at the tip. A low groan escaped from the back of my throat each time I was suddenly reminded that Casey was still banging me.

Eventually, I felt Casey's fingers exit my pussy. He lifted my ass to take my weight off his lap. Out of the corner of my eye, while maintaining the steady work of my mouth, I watched him quickly remove his pants. Then he readjusted himself on the end of the couch, moving my hips and legs so he could kneel between them. I closed my eyes and focused on exploring every shape of Ryan's penis. I felt Casey tease my pussy with the tip of his cock, soaking himself in my wetness. When he entered me, I swallowed him whole and he glided smoothly into the deepest crevice of my insides that he could reach. A sense of fulfillment shot through my body. It was as if my pussy had been dying of thirst and was finally gulping down a bottle of water. Casey gave me a few slow, gentle thrusts, but soon fell into a steady pattern of aggressive fucking. He felt like a pleasantly rough massage inside of me, the way it feels to have an elbow working away on a knot in my back. I felt like he was fucking me like he meant it, and I liked that. I wanted it harder and faster, and he gave it to me that way.

My body wanted to focus solely on the excitement flowing through my vagina. My breathing became heavier and I almost felt light-headed. I struggled to maintain my aggression and determination on Ryan's cock, but soon my head collapsed flat onto the cushions. But Ryan didn't seem to mind and didn't even skip a beat. He readjusted himself, inserting his penis back between my lips and bracing his weight with his arms on the back of the couch. He thrust his hips so I no longer needed to strain my neck to blow him. All I had to do was suck.

Soon, the three of us slipped into a synchronized dance. Casey and Ryan gyrated their hips to the same beat and at the same speed. I lay there, happy to be the center of attention, and consumed both of them eagerly. Both ends of my body were being pleasured in the best ways. The sexual energy from the boys met in the middle and collided in my stomach. A titillating and dangerous sensation developed within me, as if I were spiraling to the ground on the vertical drop of a rollercoaster. We moaned and groaned and panted together, no one needing to push or shove to be a part of. I strained to watch my body succumb to both men and thought that we looked more titillating than the girls in the video. But once we had maintained a consistent rhythm of fucking for a while, the intense shocks exploding within me began to dull. My legs and back grew sore and my pussy soon became dry. I needed to change positions.

Without a word, I hastily pulled myself away from both boys. I turned onto my hands and knees, facing Casey. Then I vacuumed his erection into my mouth and returned to work. He was slightly longer than Ryan, but at the same time, a bit thinner. I found that I could not quite reach the base of his cock without risking a gag or cough. So I focused on my pressure, sucking mostly on the head hard enough to cause my cheeks to cramp. I could taste myself on his skin. My vagina's saliva was both a little sweet and a little sour. Casey moved to sit on the arm of the couch. I moved with him, to keep him in my mouth, and supported myself with my arms on his thighs. I arched my back and stretched my shoulders to present my ass high in the air. The moment I had readjusted, I felt Ryan lather my pussy with his hand, which he must have spit into. Then he pushed himself inside of me. His hips slammed into my ass with each forward thrust. I could feel the tip of his cock visiting different tunnels within me, ones that Casey was unable to enter when I was on my back. I rocked back and forth, in sync with Ryan. When he pushed forward, I pushed my hips back to force him deeper into me. My head fell into the same pace and timing to allow my mouth to travel up and down Casey's penis. And again, the three of us danced, on beat and in harmony. Occasionally, Ryan would slip out of my pussy and enter my asshole. At first, his intrusion sent a sharp pain through my lower body. But my wetness had lubricated his cock and my ass gradually opened up to accept it. And he alternated between my vagina and my anus, fucking one, then the other, until I finally collapsed flat on my stomach in complete exhaustion.

I declared that I needed another line and the boys agreed. The porn on the television had ended and was repeating the crude clip on the DVD menu over and over. I retrieved the cocaine, cutting lines for all of us, but snorting mine first. We fell back onto the couch, sitting in a row, me sandwiched in the middle again. We casually talked about sex and how impossible it is to orgasm with blow in our systems. None of us had come, but none of us had expected to. And we were all perfectly satisfied with the impromptu dance we had performed together.

By the time the sun had risen, the boys had passed out on each other's shoulders, having never moved from the couch. I had remained awake, finishing the drugs and desperately crawling around on the floor in search of additional remnants. I was coming down bad and it only got worse. When my search became hopeless, I let myself out of the apartment and walked back to the bar where my car sat waiting. I stumbled inside and began the trek across town to get ready for work.

Nearly a month had passed when the fifth day arrived. It came unexpectedly because, although I had seen Lucas around, he remained cold and refused to be left alone with me. I assumed he had heard through the grapevine about my night with Casey and Ryan. But I had ceased feeling guilty about my promiscuity. And I had thrown myself into many similar situations with various men and women since then. My attraction to Lucas and yearn to be alone with him had not decreased. But I needed sex and attention on a regular basis, regardless of whom it came from. I needed that validation.

I was at the bar, which had become my second home. It was still early, but the warmth of the alcohol in my first drink instigated a vicious craving for heavier drugs. Lucas was within easy reach, but he was busy chatting up another girl. I politely waited until she excused herself to use the restroom. The moment she was out of sight, I tenderly approached him. I bluntly asked if he had anything he could sell me. He stated that he didn't have anything on him, but had plenty at home and would retrieve it for me later. I thanked him and returned to my drink. Two rum and Cokes later, Lucas and the girl appeared to be departing company. I was unable to read them or guess the status of their relationship. I had heard through mutual friends that Lucas was hung up on a girl who did not share the same level of interest in him. Perhaps that was her.

This time, he came to me. He asked if I still wanted a hook-up. When I said I did, he invited me to go with him to get it. I was taken aback by the offer, but hastily agreed. I climbed onto the back of his motorcycle, slipped on the spare helmet he kept in the storage bin, and rode with him to his father's house where he still lived. We didn't exchange a word. When we pulled into the driveway, the dogs immediately began barking. I had been to the house several times before, which I was told by others was a big deal. Lucas was very selective about who he brought home. He was more likely to shell out the cash for a motel room than bring casual acquaintances to his father's territory.

When we entered the house, Lucas quieted the dogs—a Husky, a German Shepherd, and a blind Chihuahua. All was dark. We tip-toed through the living room, down the hallway, and into his bedroom. I could hear the television through the walls and assumed his father had secluded to his own room for the night. Lucas' room consisted of a bed, a dresser with a television propped on top of it and a closet.

Clothes, trash, and cases containing unregistered guns littered the stained carpet. I dropped my purse, removed my shoes, and sat patiently on the bed. Lucas remained silent as he retrieved a large bag of cocaine from his top dresser drawer. The bag must have been a purchase from his own connection because it held at least a grand worth of drugs which was still in rock form rather than powder. He selected a single rock, joined me on the bed, and began cutting it up on a CD case. He offered me the first two lines then snorted his own. A drawn out minute passed as we waited for the effects. Once it hit us, he finally began talking. He apologized for avoiding me the past few weeks. He explained that we were growing too close too fast. He knew that I wanted to be his girlfriend and that made him uncomfortable. And I had embarrassed him more than once at the bar by getting wasted and causing a scene. I apologized for making him uncomfortable and admitted that I had missed him. He said that he missed me too, and was happy that I had agreed to come over. We spoke for hours about life—past, present and future. We slipped into a drug-induced philosophical debate. He kept cutting more lines and we kept snorting them. He never asked me to pay for it and I never offered. As our energy diminished and the night grew colder, we laid down together, our arms wrapped around one another. He told me that he was scared, and that he didn't want to hurt people anymore. A hint of moisture developed in his eyes creating a glassy replica of the ocean's lullaby at low tide. I whispered in his ear to comfort him. I told him everything would be okay. Then I leaned in to kiss him and we made love as if we had never been apart.

Looking back, it wasn't love that we made. It was simply sex, maybe even pure fucking. And it was exactly the same as the first time and every time in between. I climbed on top of him, straddling his hips. I forced him inside of me and rocked back and forth on my knees or bounced up and down when I adjusted onto my feet. He laid there, flat on his back, eyes closed, hands gently placed on my waist. The act was more of a work-out than anything else for me. But again, I didn't mind—I only wanted to pleasure him. When he came, I collapsed on top of him, keeping him inside of me until his cock slowly deflated and slipped out on its own. And soon he fell asleep. I watched him laying there. He still looked distraught, even as he slumbered. Unable to keep still myself, I finished the drugs he had set out for us and quietly, carefully stole another small amount from his stash in the dresser. Finally, in the early afternoon of the next day, Lucas awoke. He drove me back to my car and we departed ways.

The sixth day arrived exactly one week later. Lucas had warmed up to me just slightly again. He was spending less and less time at the bar and with the usual guys like Casey and Ryan. Instead, he was socializing with his older friends, both in age and time, people he had known for at least half a decade. His best friend, Dean, was a ragged man in his early fifties who had spent several years of his youth fighting in Vietnam. Lucas was happy to let me tag along with him again, but it meant going to new places and meeting new people. That night, we trekked just a few miles northwest to a three-story condo somewhere between Brentwood and Westwood. This was where Dean lived. I was welcomed graciously with wine and cheese and crackers. We sat on bar stools around a blue tiled island in the kitchen. A large flat screen TV was embedded into a nearby wall and was tuned to a digital radio station playing ambient beats through invisible surround sound speakers. I mostly smiled and nodded while the men chatted about war and guns and the military. I felt too naïve about the subject matter to pipe in, but considered their words mature and intelligent. I suddenly appreciated being in the company of older, wiser men for a change. Of course, the lines came out and were distributed freely. Dean preferred to smoke, mixing the rocks with baking soda, briefly popping it in the microwave, then loading it into a thin metal pipe. He saw that I was mostly being left out of their conversations and occasionally turned to me to inquire about my life and interests and endeavors. And that night, for those first few hours, I felt unfamiliarly connected to these other human beings who were both so different from myself. I felt like I was experiencing the most beautiful aspect of human cognition. And I felt like I belonged.

Somewhere in the late hours of the night or the early hours of the morning, there came a knock on the front door. Dean rose to answer it and a young woman I had never seen before pushed past him and entered the kitchen. She was tall and curvy with golden brown skin and exotic features. She must have been in her late twenties. She wore a short, tight skirt that accentuated her long, smooth legs and wide hips, and a thin cut of material that may have been considered a halter top and showed off her plump, bouncy cleavage. She was plastered and stumbled in, loud and barely intelligible. The moment she entered, a sort of tenseness came over the room. Dean looked worried, like he didn't have the energy to deal with this unexpected situation. Lucas looked irritated. The woman over-enthusiastically introduced herself to me as Gina. I offered my hand but she pulled me in for a sloppy, tight hug. Then she approached Lucas at the counter and helped herself to a line. She clasped Lucas' head in both her hands and continuously kissed every pore on his face. She explained that she just knew he would be here, how happy she was to have found him, and how she missed him so much that she was contemplating suicide. Then she grabbed him by the hand and began to lead him upstairs. He protested at first, but decided it was safer to play her little game and trudged up the stairs. He briefly turned back to throw Dean some sort of coded glance. Once they were out of sight, Dean turned to me and explained the Gina was Lucas' ex-girlfriend. Apparently the two of them had maintained a chaotic on-and-off relationship over the past four years. Lucas was still deeply in love with her, but she was the one who constantly cheated or broke up with him. Sometimes she would simply disappear and lose contact with Lucas and all their mutual friends for months at a time. Those times were the easiest. But sometimes she would reappear out of nowhere, usually wasted and always expressing melodramatic apologies and desires to get back together. Her uninvited entrance that night was something that had happened before—more than once.

Dean collected the cocaine and paraphernalia then gestured for me to follow him upstairs. Unsure of my other options, I obeyed. He led me into the bedroom, which was a huge, wide open space with a ceiling forty feet high. Almost everything in the room was a blinding pure white—the walls, the carpet, the bed spread, the couch. Anything that wasn't white was wood and stained a chocolate brown—the bed frame, a dresser, a bookshelf. Another immense flat screen television hung on the wall where it could be enjoyed from in bed. One wall was entirely made up of floor-to-ceiling windows lined with thin, white curtains. There was an iron spiral staircase leading to the third floor of the condo, which looked down into the bedroom. I heard voices from within the room but saw no one. Dean further led me just past the staircase and into a bathroom the size of my entire studio apartment. Half of the bathroom was a deep Jacuzzi bath tub, large enough to fit six people. The water was already running and Gina stood naked in the tub, begging Lucas to join her. She had the body of a true woman, unlike me, who mostly still looked like a little girl. Even without her push-up bra, her breasts remained large and perky. Her ass was plump, bronze, and perfectly symmetrical. Her pelvis was freshly shaved, completely bare and smooth. There wasn't a single inch of her body that I didn't yearn to touch.

When Dean and I made our appearance known, Gina invited us to join her as well. Both intimidated and intrigued by my new found competition, I promptly accepted. Highly intoxicated myself, I hastily removed all my clothing and climbed into the tub. I was momentarily self-conscious of my body in comparison to hers, so I quickly sat down where I felt less exposed under the water. I was relieved that, I too, had shaved just the night before.

Lucas and Dean exchanged another private look before reluctantly undressing themselves. I was already familiar with Lucas' body—toned, except for the slightest hint of a youthful beer belly, and largely covered in dramatic ink, which served him well. Dean, on the other hand, was much older, and looked it. He was thin, but his aged skin had long since begun to sag from his bones. He was wrinkled and crooked, and the faded tattoos on both his arms were no longer intelligible. They joined us in the tub, Lucas next to me and Dean next to Gina. There was an extremely awkward tension in the air, which everybody seemed to notice, except for Gina. She continued in her slurred chattiness, first describing how wonderful the hot water felt against her skin, then further explaining why this was exactly what she needed. She narrated the details of her most recent dramas as a highly successful physical therapist, including how all her male clients were constantly asking her out. She specifically replayed the conversations she'd had during a highly romantic and expensive date with a popular television actor, and how she'd turned him down after the second date when she learned that he was married. While she spoke, the rest of us listened, or at least pretended to listen. I kept sensing that something bad was about to happen, and in some sick way, I was looking forward to it. But I wasn't prepared for the emotions that would come with it. One minute, everything was fine—awkward, but fine. Then the next, I felt as if I was sinking into the depths of the ocean with cinderblocks strapped to my ankles, the circle of sunlight from above progressively getting smaller and smaller.

Gina crawled to Lucas until they were face to face. She wrapped her arms around his neck, her bare chest pressed against his, then planted a sensual, seductive kiss on his lips. He let her do it, but didn't respond. It wasn't until she continued in a more forceful manner, that he gently pushed her away and told her to stop. Which she did. But then she slipped herself behind him, until he was sitting between her legs, his back leaning against her torso. She massaged his neck, working her professional fingers into his tense muscles. And he began to relax, allowing himself to give into her touch, occasionally releasing soft moans of pleasure.

At first, I froze, unsure of whether I was feeling hurt or jealous, or both. So I turned my head and looked in another direction, staring at the white lines between the blue tiles lining the wall just above the tub. I couldn't help but look back at them when I heard an intensified sound escape from Lucas' throat. At first glance, nothing seemed to have changed. But then I realized that she had wrapped one of her fists around his hardened cock, and was gently stroking it.

Instinctually, I rose and stepped out of the tub. I grabbed the first towel that I could and exited into the bedroom, hastily drying myself off as I walked. I collapsed on the bed, still damp. I wanted to hit or throw something, but my muscles locked up and shot my anger further inside of me rather than out. I noticed the cocaine had been left on the night stand next to me and snorted directly from the mound without bothering to cut lines. Then I heard the sound of splashing water and footsteps as another body exited the tub and came after me. Out of the corner of my eye, I saw that it was Dean. My disappointment caused my chest to tighten and I grew light-headed. But I accepted his presence and was relieved when he didn't talk. Instead, he climbed onto the bed next to me, keeping just enough distance so we weren't touching. I ignored him and inhaled another overdose of powder. Then I lay on my back and blinked at the perfectly pale white ceiling high above me. Several minutes of silence passed. Dean still did not speak. I could tell he was waiting for me to say something first. But I had nothing to say. I couldn't intellectualize what was going on inside me and definitely couldn't put it into words. So finally, he laid on his side next to me, propping up his head with his hand and his elbow on the pillow. He began to run his fingers through my hair, sending a pleasant tingle through my scalp. At first I wanted to push him away. I didn't want him, I wanted Lucas. But then I realized that what I really wanted, in that moment, was a man's touch, regardless of who it came from.

I remained still and unresponsive, but allowed Dean to continue running his hands across me. He dragged his fingertips along my skin, respectfully avoiding my breasts and sliding between them, then down to my stomach. His barely-there touch relaxed me, allowing me to breathe normally again and causing my muscles to loosen. Eventually, he leaned into me and came in for a kiss. I finally reacted to him by quickly turning away. He didn't seem offended by my denial and didn't make a second attempt. Instead, he sat up and moved down to the end of the bed by my ankles. He continued tracing his fingers down my legs then across the bottoms of my feet. Then he worked his way back up, focusing his touch on my thighs and stomach, staying outside the perimeter of my crotch. Something about Dean made me feel dirty, causing a lump in my throat. But his hands felt so warm and gentle and soothing. My head kept telling me to say "no" but my body wouldn't allow my lips to part. Instead, I just laid there, paralyzed, a breathing corpse.

Suddenly, without a sound or warning, Lucas collapsed onto the bed, laying parallel to me. He briefly glanced over at me and we caught eyes, as if to ask my permission to be there. I granted it by looking away and back up at the ceiling. Within my peripheral vision, I watched Gina climb on top of him, straddling him, forcing him inside of her. She rocked back and forth on his cock, in exactly the same way that he and I had done it so many times. And it dawned on me that this must be the only way that Lucas ever had sex, and that the way he and I had done it was nothing special.

Watching them had caused me to completely forget about Dean. I suddenly realized that he was eating me out and I wondered how long he'd been down there. But as soon as I re-acknowledged his presence, I realized that a completely euphoric sensation was bouncing through every pore and crevice between my legs. His tongue was thick and warm and fluttered consistently fast without too much pressure. My increased pulse throbbed in my vagina so hard that I was certain he could feel it. He licked me in areas that had never excited me before, but suddenly they reacted as if this were the first time I had ever been gone down on. I felt an orgasm growing within me, but held it back. I didn't want to come, but I wasn't sure why. Perhaps it was because Lucas had never made me come and there he was, lying right next to me. Or perhaps it was because I found Dean so unattractive that I felt disgusted by the idea of letting him pleasure me. Regardless, I couldn't tell him to stop.

I flexed every muscle in my body, trying to hold the orgasm in. But the moment that Dean reached up to gently rub my nipples with his fingers, I exploded. I flailed through the strongest orgasm I had experienced in longer than I could remember. I screamed out, louder than I wanted, pulling tightly on the sheets and kicking the mattress below. When Dean didn't immediately cease licking me, I kicked him hard in the shoulder to push him away. He climbed on top of me and shoved his erection between my legs. I cried out when a sharp pain shot from inside of me and up to my head. His cock was large, too large, and rammed into tunnels in my body that had never been explored before. But I let him grind into me, my eyes watering until I became completely numb and I could no longer even feel him. I could see his face bouncing above me. Gravity forced his wrinkled, loose skin to hang low and I noticed for the first time that his teeth were so unaligned that they overlapped one another. I had to look away and, instead, returned my focus to Gina, who had increased her speed as she rode Lucas. Beads of sweat made her tan skin glisten in the dim light. Her breasts bounced up and down and her dark hair was matted against her neck. I strained to see Lucas' face. Like always, his eyes were closed.

The men must have come at the same time as Dean and Gina both collapsed onto us simultaneously. I pushed Dean off of me, no longer wanting to be touched by anyone. But then I found myself paralyzed again. I was still flat on my back and couldn't find the strength to change that. So I slowly allowed me eyes to shut.

I woke in the exact same position as the blaring sun was just seeping through the curtains. As if a vampire, I leaped out of the bed and hurried to the side of the room that was still shadowed. I found that I was alone. I collected my clothes from the bathroom and dressed. I stumbled downstairs to find Dean in the kitchen, cooking me breakfast. He said that Lucas and Gina had both left several hours ago, while I was asleep. With nothing better to do, I sat myself at the counter, and forced down a plate of bacon and eggs.

A month passed before the seventh day came. I had stopped going to the bar altogether and spent almost all of my time outside of work at Dean's condo. I couldn't comprehend how it had happened, but I was practically living with him. I stayed there most nights, only running home occasionally to collect clean clothes. He served me dinner and breakfast every time I was over and hooked me up with cheap, if not free, cocaine. Occasionally we'd go out for a drink together, but for the most part, we stayed in, watching movies and playing backgammon. In a matter of a few weeks, I had become his pretty, little pet.

I had not seen nor spoken to Lucas whatsoever since the night in the bath tub. Lucas and Dean were best friends and I couldn't fathom what they could possibly be saying about me to one another. Dean was perfectly aware that I was still hung up on Lucas. I shared about our scattered pseudo-relationship often, somehow hoping that he could help me win Lucas back. At first, Dean kept me optimistic, assuring me that Lucas simply needed some time to himself but would eventually return to his senses and beg for my attention again. But soon, Dean's tactics seemed to change. He began describing Lucas' many faults to me, things he claimed only he knew. He told me that Lucas was regularly going over to Gina's for "physical therapy" and that the two of them were together again. And he told me that Lucas had fallen head over heels in love with a new girl, who wouldn't give him the time of day. Dean's approach was always passive-aggressive, phrasing these stories in a way that hurt me, but making them sound like he was helping me. I could see right through him, but all I did was smile and nod. I had tangled myself into an awkward, confusing web. I lost the ability to take care of myself in the simplest ways. I couldn't eat without being fed. I rarely showered and I never slept. And I was high or drunk or both almost every minute of every day. My life narrowed down to the mere fact that Dean took care of me and Lucas didn't. And that was enough.

That night, I saw Lucas for the last time. He and Dean had planned a night of bar-hopping via their motorcycles and I was invited at the last minute. I didn't hesitate to accept. Any opportunity to spend time with Lucas was an opportunity I couldn't miss. A friend of Dean's from Las Vegas was in town for the weekend and joined us. She was a Filipina woman, probably in her mid-forties, and would have been attractive if she dressed and acted more her age. Instead, her and I hit it off and spent the next several hours behaving like desperate college kids trying to land a spot on "Girls Gone Wild." We drank heavily, yelled obscenities in all directions, and fondled one another to entertain the men in every bar we hit. She went by Tara, though she openly admitted repeatedly that wasn't her real name. I was excited by her presence and the idea that her inclusion in the outing made me feel like we were all on a double-date. My excitement waned when I realized that she would be Lucas' date and I would be Dean's. But I played along, riding on the back of Dean's bike as we sped down avenues and freeways alongside Lucas, who carried Tara on his seat. By the time we made it to our final stop of the night, I had lost all comprehension of my whereabouts. I linked my hands together, my arms wrapped around Dean's waist, knowing that if I tried to move or adjust in anyway, I'd be likely to fly off the seat and skid across the pavement below. In ways, that possibility sounded appealing and freeing. But in other ways, it sounded like a hassle and a huge hospital bill. So I remained still. The chilly night breeze whipped through my hair that hung below my helmet, then down the neck of my jacket and into the waistline of my jeans. The loud roar of the engines drowned out the normal, irritating sounds of Los Angeles traffic and eventually became a mere constant hum in my ears. I felt as if I had drifted into a state of non-existence, where I was invincible and peacefully alone.

We arrived at the final bar of the night just prior to last call. It was another hole-in-the-wall, just like the others, but every seat was taken. A couple of men offered their seats to Tara and I while Lucas and Dean shifted on their feet next to us. I sipped on my tenth or eleventh mixed drink of the evening, unable to focus my eyes or sit without bracing myself against the chair back. I saw a blurry mess of colors and the movement of warm bodies. I could no longer speak, so I constrained my conversations to laughing, nodding and flailing gestures with one arm.

And then I realized that Lucas was no longer with us. He had moved to the bar where he was chatting up a lone blonde. When I inquired, Dean told me that she was the girl

Lucas had been hung up on most recently. The girl that he'd claimed he was in love with but wouldn't give him the time of day. And that was all it took to get me on my feet again. I followed Lucas and the blonde outside. She was insisting that she needed to leave. He was begging her to stay a little longer. And all the anger, resentment, jealousy and hurt that I had felt toward Lucas but had hidden inside of myself, suddenly came to the surface. I stepped between them, still drunk and still feeling invincible. I pushed Lucas in the chest, causing him to stumble backwards a step or two. Then I slapped him hard across the face. He looked more shocked and confused than anything else. I went at him again with my other arm, but he grabbed onto my wrist and held it back. I kicked at his shins and struggled to wrap my hands around his neck, but succeeded only in scratching him with my nails. He continued to back away from me until we were almost against the building. Finally, he got a solid grasp on both my arms, lifted me off the pavement and threw me against the wall. I gave up with my attack and instead, fell to the sidewalk and began to sob.

Dean had appeared at some point and I heard raised voices then, eventually, calmer conversation. I heard the engine of a motorcycle rev up then drive away and fade out into the distance. I felt Dean's hands on me as he picked me up and carried me like a small child. He sat me on the seat of his bike, made sure I was holding on tight, then drove us back to his condo. Tara had found a new man to take her home for the night.

I stayed in bed for three days straight, only rising to use the bathroom and inhale servings of cocaine that Dean had brought home for me. I called in sick to work and refused to talk. If I was high enough, I'd entertain a game of backgammon. Otherwise, I was asleep, or laying in bed, wishing I was asleep.

I was woken by a telephone ring in the early morning hours of the eighth day. It was dark, but I could see Dean's silhouette rise from the bed next to me and answer the phone. The conversation was long—too long. The person on the other end was doing all the talking, so I couldn't piece together what it was regarding. So I soon drifted back to sleep.

Dean gently shook me awake again and said he needed to go to the hospital. He explained that Lucas had been in a motorcycle accident late the night before. An anonymous 9-11 caller had informed the police and paramedics where his body could be found. The accident had occurred in the small intersection of a quiet residential neighborhood. Most of the bike was found lying against the curb of the sidewalk. A few parts broken off one side of it were scattered nearby. Lucas was found flat on his stomach more than fifty feet away. But the trail of blood on the pavement showed that he had landed slightly closer and had probably crawled the last fifteen feet before collapsing. There was no one around when the paramedics arrived—not even curious bystanders from the surrounding houses. The accident hadn't stirred anyone from their sleep. Initial viewing of the scene implied that Lucas had been driving under the influence, tried to make a left turn too fast, causing the bike to skid and fall onto its side. But it wasn't clear why Lucas had flown so far from the bike, rather than landing next to it, if not under it, like expected. And the tire skid marks leading up to the accident were also accompanied by the skid marks of a second vehicle, most likely a pick-up truck. So the police did not rule out the possibility that it may have been a hit and run.

Regardless of what happened that night, Lucas was in the hospital, in a coma, completely brain-dead. His was heart beating and his lungs were pumping only because of life-support machines and technology. Dean and I went to the hospital, but only family members were permitted inside the unit, so we spent the morning and afternoon sitting outside and walking the hospital grounds. Other friends stopped by to join us, like Casey and Ryan. We chain-smoked cigarettes, discussing the situation, what we had each heard from different sources. But Dean maintained the most updated and accurate information because he kept in constant contact with Lucas' father, who eventually shut down and stopped relaying any news after too many inquiries.

A month passed. Then two, then three. Lucas had been turned over to a university medical team and was kept on life support for research purposes only. Occasionally, small hints of hope were announced—a flash of minor brain activity, a fluttering of eyelids.

When I cut ties with Dean, I lost all access to news about Lucas. I had no way of knowing whether he was dead or alive. And I slowly thought of him less and less. Years passed and he became a distant memory. But even then, every once in a while, I would be sitting in traffic and a motorcycle would shoot past me. And I'd strain to catch a glimpse of the driver's face to see if it was Lucas. And I'd imagine that it was him and that he was alive and fully recovered. And that he was happy.

The Client

"Get naked."

I laughed, sharing his sense of humor, and slowly began
to remove my shirt.

"Okay, but I'm gonna have to charge you for that," I coyly
responded. He simply grinned and re-instructed me to lift
my shirt up so he could examine the shape and size of my
upper back.

"Yeah, the graphic should go on top, right about here," he
recommended while placing his warm, moist palm gently
between my shoulder blades. His voice had a seductive crack
to it, the kind developed from years of smoking. "And the
characters slightly smaller, right below that."

"Sounds good to me," I rushed the words, anxious to pull
my shirt back down. Something about his touch had caused
the area between my thighs to moisten. "So, about how
much will it cost?"

"The snakes alone are gonna run about $150, then
another, let's say, $80 for the Japanese." As he spoke, he
slowly lowered himself to a kneeling position and finished
his sentence looking up at me. An imaginary breeze seemed
to tease the hem of my skirt. I placed my palms on the sides
of my thighs in order to prevent the material from giving
him a free peep show.

After a brief, uncomfortable break in the conversation, I
lowered myself to his level and gently leaned the bulk of my

weight against a nearby wall. Our knees momentarily bumped against each other. He smiled. I returned the gesture but quickly averted my eyes to the floor. I wasn't usually uncomfortable making business negotiations with a good-looking man, even if it was obvious he was desperately coming onto me. But something about him made me blush. I guess he was good like that. Without hesitation, he slipped his hand under my skirt. I slapped it away, the same way a mother slaps her son's hand when he's caught sneaking into the cookie jar before dinner.

"Hey," I warned, "Don't get too excited. Like I said, I usually charge for that."

"Really?" he whispered. "Well, maybe we could work out a deal."

I hungrily swallowed the seductive look in his eyes and the subtle twitch at the corner of his mouth. A part of me simply wanted to blurt out, "Sure!" but in that moment, I refused to come off as a mere tease. I needed to make sure that he understood that I meant business.

"Maybe," I whispered back, "We'll see."

Damien was the first man I ever fucked on business terms for something other than cash or drugs. However, the transaction was similar, as I was providing a service in order to get a discount on a product. The primary difference with this transaction compared to others from my past was that this time, I didn't need it. I didn't need to fuck anybody to get a damn thing—not anymore. But for some unexplainable reason, I sure as hell still wanted to.

"So, now what?" I asked, briefly breaking the sexual tension.

"Well, there's a forty dollar deposit to do the sketch, but that'll come out of the total cost of the tattoo when you come back to get the actual work done."

I let my purse fall from my shoulder into my hand. I opened my wallet and began flipping through bills. I handed Damien two twenties, but not before indiscreetly exposing the three C-notes at the bottom of the stack. I never carried too much money around, which probably explained why large amounts of cash under my possession were such a turn-on to me. I also was never the type to show-off the cash I did have. But this time, I was pretty grandiose about the $300 plus I had on me. Perhaps I simply wanted to hint to Damien that I didn't need a discount, but rather that I actually wanted to know what his fingers, his tongue, his cock, would feel like inside of me.

"So, let's set an appointment. What's good for you?" Damien asked.

"About how long will it take?"

"It depends. That top part will take at least an hour alone. So maybe two hours or so. But if you're moving around a lot, you know, trying to pull away from the needle, it could take up to four."

"It'll have to be a weekend, then." I leaned in close to his neck to get an upside-down glance at his appointment book. I intentionally exhaled into his ear. He moaned, but played it off as if responding to a note on his calendar. After a couple back and forth conflicted dates, he finally jotted my name and number on a Sunday afternoon, about a week and a half away.

"Cool, so we'll see each other then." Damien threw his arm around my waist and pulled me in close as he walked me to the door. He kept a hold on me as I stepped out into the warm wind outside. I was startled when he pulled me back into his body.

"See you then," he softly whispered into my ear, his breath teasing my neck. I pulled away, leaving him only with a vague grin over my shoulder. As I walked toward the parking lot, I could feel his gaze following me. I could also still feel a hint of hardness through his jeans, which had teased my lower back before he had released me. I toyed with two possible descriptions of that hardness—either he'd be quick and easy, or he'd be sexually dominant and potentially difficult.

Any girl who tells you she doesn't prefer the latter is lying.

The Sunday of my appointment came quickly. I was nervous, being my first tattoo, so I brought my best friend, Shawn with me. Damien was running late, so Shawn and I killed time smoking cigarettes, flipping through the portfolios on display, and immaturely making fun of one another. I immediately blushed when Damien rushed in, apologizing for his tardiness. He glanced at Shawn, obviously concerned that I had brought a male friend with me. He required a little more time in order to prepare, but I knew I would be satisfied with the results as soon as I saw the sketch blue-printed onto my back. There was something undoubtedly erotic about the whole procedure. I was told to sit backwards on a metal folding chair. In order to comfortably place my feet flat on the floor, I had to completely straddle my legs. I felt the metal bar of the chair tuck itself directly between my thighs. I chose not to readjust. I was then told to bend over the back of the chair, letting my head and hair hang toward the floor. I kept my bra and hip-hugger jeans on, but could feel my thin, black thong exposing itself as my belt-less pants struggled to remain situated. I could not see him behind me, but I could feel Damien bring his rolling chair closer. He kept his foot on the pedal of a nearby trash can as he prepped the necessary tools and supplies. Every time I heard the trash can open and shut, I felt him bring his chair even closer. By the time he was ready to start, he was so close to me, I could feel his cock through both of our pants, resting against the top of my ass. He squeezed his legs tight around me, holding my body still. He wrapped his left arm around my waist and placed his hand on my stomach. Damien's touch, as well as the part of the chair between my legs, caused my vagina to throb. My face and neck flushed. I quickly glanced up at Shawn, who was watching from outside the room, making sure he hadn't noticed how turned on I had already become. He would never let me hear the end of it. Fortunately, he didn't seem to, and instead taunted me with, "It's gonna hurt. You know I just came to see you scream." Shawn shot me a mischievous grin as I flipped him the bird.

"He came to see you make some faces," Damien agreed.

I held still, determined to prove them wrong and to get the work done as quickly as possible. Finally, I heard the quiet buzz of the needle start up. I refused to let my muscles tense and instead focused on the warmth of Damien's legs against mine and the dampness of his palm on my waist.

The beginning stages of my first tattoo were surprisingly easy. I felt only a slight sting, as if a sharp blade was slowly tracing the design imprinted on my back. I suddenly recalled a moment from my past where I had been tied up with a belt and a young man gently pressed the pointed end of a switch blade against the lips of my vagina, and then slowly dragged it from the tip of my clitoris to the edge of my asshole. The erotic rush was so intense that it traveled from the inner most area of my body to the rear of my back and down to my calves. I felt as if a sensual vibration was teasing every nerve in my body. For a moment, I thought I was at home, lying in bed alone, with my favorite bunny-eared toy fully fledged by four AA batteries.

Like I said, there is definitely something undeniably erotic about getting a tattoo. Especially when it's one's first time. There's something about the fast motion of the needle. Something about the artist who is guiding that needle across one's body. Perhaps it's the power that the artist has over the client in that moment.

Shawn remained spectator for the first half hour or so, then excused himself for lunch. The moment he exited, the needle paused and I felt two large, warm arms wrap tightly around my waist.

"Hey," Damien's soft voice bounced against my ear drum. "I thought we were supposed to hang out."

"We are," I replied.

Damien leaned in closer, allowing the weight of his upper body to rest against my naked back. He slid his hands from my waist down to my thighs. Then he slickly snuck his fingers between my legs and teased me through the crotch of my jeans. I could feel his warm breath become heavier. I could feel the pores across my body inhale every discharge of carbon dioxide he released.

Suddenly, a shout from one of his employees startled us both and caused Damien to abruptly pull away.

"Phone call!" the employee announced, passing a cell to Damien.

"Tattoos," Damien greeted the caller. I listen to the conversation, only catching bits and pieces, anxious for it to end. The employee left the room, but the call continued. Damien used his free hand to slowly unzip my jeans. I shifted to make it easier for him, but remained relaxed, as if his actions were a perfectly normal addition to his artistic services.

"Well, the work has already been done, so I can't give you a refund," he spoke into the phone. "But we can schedule a time for you to come back and I'll re-pierce it for you."

My jeans were successfully opened and welcomed Damien's hand. My wetness had already soaked through to the exterior of my underwear. Damien struggled momentarily to slip his index and middle fingers around the inner hem of my panties. He teased my clit, barely caressing the tip of it with one finger. He inserted his other finger inside of me and began to rock his hand back and forth. I couldn't help but release a quiet moan.

"Hey!" Damien called out to the front desk. "Grab my appointment book."

Damien gave my clit one last pinch then smoothly retracted his hand from between my thighs. The employee returned with the thin, black book. He handed it to Damien, who quickly made a short note then handed it back.

"Thanks."

The employee took this as his cue to leave and I heard the needle resume its sensual buzz. I remained motionless as I felt Damien filling in the color of my tattoo. The pain increased from a sort of gentle love-making to a desperate fuck. A part of me wanted to pull away, but the other part wanted the needle to dive in even deeper.

Without warning, the buzz of the needle ceased. Damien grabbed me by the waist and lifted me to a standing position.

"Come here," he demanded under his breath. He grabbed my hand and led me out of the room into the slim hallway after looking both ways for clientele traffic. He pulled me into a back room, leaving the door open so the bathroom at the end of the hall remained accessible. The area was dimly lit by a single bulb and minimally stocked with unopened boxes. Against one wall was a sort of bench or bed, much like one a woman is asked to lay on when she goes to the clinic for her annual pap smear. It was coated with brown leather and carried a thin layer of dust.

My jeans were still unzipped. Damien removed them and my panties in one swift maneuver. I kicked the clothing off from around my ankles. He grabbed my shoulders tightly, pulled me hard into his body, and wrapped his lips around mine. He tasted like bitter honey—sweet but containing enough tang to spark my interest. His tongue felt warm and soft against mine. We teased each other—licking, sucking, biting. Without hesitation, he shoved his fingers into my pussy, pressing hard, forcing them in as deep as possible. I cupped my hand around the crotch of his pants, searching frantically for his hardness. Once I found it, I felt it grow. Our breathing became heavier, sounding almost as if we were under water. Damien dropped to his knees and lifted his chin so his mouth was perfectly wrapped around the entirety of my wetness. His tongue moved fast. He primarily used the tip, applying just enough pressure to tease but not torture. His pace never slowed. Occasionally, he'd up the ante by slowly dragging his entire tongue across my clit. Then he would shove it inside of me, sampling every pore, tasting every crevice. He picked me up and laid me down on the leather bed. My legs remained spread, my back arched. I could feel my juices dripping from my cunt to my ass, and eventually onto the brown leather.

"Get naked," he demanded. I immediately obliged, frantically stripping the clothes that remained on me. Damien rushed to the door, shut it, and balanced a nearby stool against the knob for extra measure. When he was done setting up the precautions, he forcefully widened my straddle and continued the task he had begun. As he directed my body back and forth with his hands, my head repeatedly bumped against the wall. I arched my back as much as I could and assisted in the gyrations with my arms behind me. I watched him suck me, lick me, eat me. I watched how quickly his tongue was moving. I focused on his warm, fast breath hitting my skin. His skills were good. No, his skills were fantastic. I allowed my head to bump against the wall again in order to lick my own fingers and play with my nipples. I rubbed myself, gently circling around my cold, hard bumps, and became wetter and wetter. I could feel a puddle of my insides expanding on the bed. I wanted to come, but I didn't want him to stop. The moans I had been holding back due to the employees and clients on the other side of the wall suddenly escaped my lips unwillingly. My throat and mouth had grown dry. My gasps were short and shallow. My pussy throbbed. My muscles flexed. My legs began to shake. Damien pulled away and stepped back so he could undress himself. He tore his wife beater off and threw it behind him. He sloppily unbuckled his pants and dropped his boxers. All that remained were his socks. I licked my own fingers again and played with my pussy to keep it alive and ready. Damien's cock was impressively large—both long and thick. I eyed it hungrily, but waited for his dominance to direct it. He grabbed my hips and roughly pulled me down the bed to bring me closer. Without hesitation, he shoved himself inside of me. This time there was no teasing, no slow at first, no nothing. He fucked me hard. His thighs slapped against the side of the bed as he forced himself deep enough to hit the barriers within me. His cock expanded to every corner of my opening, and every tunnel within me. As his speed increased, so did the sound of our grunts and moans. My body hitting the wall created a rhythmic percussion. I could hear voices from the other side, discussing, laughing.

"He shut the door, so I don't know."

"What position you think they're in?"

"That's fuckin' hard core, man."

Having already failed at keeping quiet, Damien and I allowed ourselves to forget about discretion. He grabbed me again, this time in order to flip me over. My feet were back on the ground and my body leaned over the edge of the bed. Damien positioned himself behind me and lowered his center to mine. I had to stand on my toes to make the entrance as pleasurable as possible for us both. He pounded me so hard that I left hand marks in the leather. I clawed at the material, reaching for anything solid to keep me stable and standing. My moaning became uncontrollable while his turned into the repeated gasp of my name. I loved the way he said my name. I loved the way he kept repeating it. I loved the way I satisfied him and he satisfied me.

"I'm gonna come," he grunted, "Oh God, I'm gonna come."

Damien fucked me until he couldn't take it any longer. He flipped me over onto my back again, gave me one last pound, then pulled out and finished himself off with his own hand. His liquid escaped his cock, some dripping down the side, the bulk of it landing gracefully below my belly button. His juices felt magically warm and thick. He released one last grunt followed by one last squirt, then fell on top of me. He held me close. He held me tight. He kissed me hard, cleansing my mouth with his. We laid there together for a moment, catching our breath. The voices from the other room had either ceased or decreased to a whisper.

"We should get back out there," I proposed.

Damien nodded in agreement and stood up. I quickly did the same. We both relocated our clothes and began to get dressed. I was quickly back in my jeans and tank top and patiently waited for him to get settled. Once he straightened up his shirt and hair, he grabbed a bottle of 409 from one of the dark shelves. He sprayed down the bed and wiped it clean with a paper towel. I stepped back, feeling like a mature woman and a little girl at the same time. Damien placed the stool back where it belonged, opened the door, and gestured for me to exit first. As we made our way through the hallway, back to the room, I glanced at a couple of clients patiently waiting in the front. I wondered how long they had been there.

"Let me take care of them," Damien said, "I'll be back in a minute."

"No problem," I replied. I sat back down on the cold, metal chair, and resumed my proper position. I laid my head down, closed my eyes, and waited for his return.

I heard the gentle buzz of the needle, but it was the prick and longevity of it that woke me. I looked up to find that Shawn had returned from lunch and was watching intensely.

"It looks fuckin' tight," Shawn commented. "I really like the shading you did in the snakes, man."

"One more color and we're done," Damien responded.

"How'd she do?"

"Really well, actually. It's been pretty quick, cause she hasn't really been moving at all."

"Cool."

I listened to Damien and Shawn shoot the shit for the last few minutes of the procedure. I was in a bit of a euphoric but lazy state.

"Done." Damien announced. "You're free."

I stood, my legs weak from sitting so long—or perhaps from our rendezvous less than an hour prior. I examined the work on my back in the mirror as best I could. I was more than pleased.

Damien coated the fresh tattoo with lotion then covered it with Saran wrap. He gave me some quick instructions then put his arm around me and walked me to the front counter. Shawn said his good-byes and stepped outside. I lingered behind and turned to Damien.

"So, do I get a discount," I inquired.

"Of course," he replied.

I had paid cash for the work in advance, so Damien pulled out a small stack of bills and returned them to me.

"We should do this again," he added.

"Sure. I'll swing by sometime."

I gave him one final vague smile before exiting the tattoo parlor. As I walked toward the parking lot with Shawn, I could feel Damien's gaze following me. I recalled his hands, his tongue, his cock, and placed it all in a safe, secret section of my memory.

"That took a long time," Shawn interrupted my thoughts.

"Yeah?"

"Yeah. I don't know. I mean, I went home for lunch, so I didn't expect him to still be working on it when I got back. It just seemed to take longer than normal."

"Hmm," I smiled to myself, "I wonder why."

The Addict

My pimp despised being called a pimp. He considered himself a hustler, a player, a money-maker. He was never shy to admit that he was a drug dealer, a criminal, a gangster. He called himself anything but a pimp. But the bottom line was, once I came into the picture, that's exactly what he became. And, of course, I fell in love with him. At least I thought I did.

My first professional date was forty-five minutes of toying with relentless coke-dick for a hundred bucks plus tip. The client was a middle-aged African-American man, and the nephew of some has-been movie star. In the beginning, we casually conversed while snorting lines off a cracked mirror in my pimp's three-bedroom apartment. The room reeked of stale marijuana and testosterone. I straddled the client, first rubbing his shoulders, then his back, then his crotch. When we retreated to the bedroom, we took the remaining powder with us. I struggled for the first fifteen minutes, desperately sucking on a limp dick that had been long knocked unconscious by a weekend of obvious drug use and masturbation. When it became apparent that sex wasn't an option, we licked, we sucked, we sixty-nined. The bedroom door had been left slightly ajar, so the client paused briefly to shut and lock it.

"Leave the door open!" The stubborn yell of my pimp startled us both. "For the safety of my lady-friend, I have to ask you to leave it open."

The client reluctantly obliged and we continued our session. I prayed that our time was almost up. I begged my so-called God to let it end. For me, it was never about the money. It was always about the sex—the undeniable fact that I loved getting fucked. Since it was obvious I wasn't going to get fucked that night, I was anxious for the experience to be over.

"Five more minutes!" his voice interrupted again.

"What? That's it?" the client whined.

"You guys have been in there for forty-five minutes. So do what you gotta do and come outta there."

Because there wasn't much left to do, or much that could be done, the client and I merely cuddled for those final minutes.

"I'm sorry," he whispered in my ear. His breath smelled so sour I almost gagged. "It's not you, it's the coke."

No shit. But I didn't say it aloud.

There was an intense banging on the bedroom door. The client and I decided it would be best to get dressed and call it a night.

When I came out of the bedroom, a hot shower was already running for me. By the time I was finished cleansing myself of his dirtiness, the client had already left. Needless to say, he had failed to leave a tip.

I joined my pimp on the couch in the living room, my hair still dripping wet. We sat together in awkward silence.

"Do you need a hug?" he finally turned to me.

I nodded and crawled onto his lap. His arms could have wrapped around me twice. He held me tight. I felt like I could have suffocated right then and died happy. And I loved the way he smelled. I always fell for men who smelled good.

We cuddled on the couch together watching Japanese anime. This particular DVD was extraordinarily erotic.

Monsters finger-banged unconscious women, who looked like combinations of porcelain China dolls and American porn stars. I felt the area between my legs moisten. My pimp had fallen asleep, so I gently shook him. He slowly lifted one eyelid, then the other. I stared at him, my own eyes droopy, my bottom lip pushed out, looking much like a young child who's been denied dessert after dinner.

"What's the matter, baby doll?" he asked.

"I'm horny," I pouted.

He seemed a bit taken aback by my bluntness, but masked it well with a cocky grin. "Well, I can take care of that. Come closer."

I was already cuddled up like a kitten on top of him, so I nuzzled my face against his neck, inhaling deeply. He began to caress my back and arms—gently at first, then eventually pinching and grabbing. I rubbed his chest and licked the outer circumference of his earlobe. He sucked on my neck, causing flutters in my stomach. He pulled at the bottom of my tight, white wife-beater, but part of the material was trapped between our bodies.

"Take this off," he murmured.

I obeyed. I was already braless and pressed my breasts hard against his chest. My school girl skirt and lacy, black panties were beginning to shift into uncomfortable places. He pinched one of my nipples, hard, just the way I liked it. I began to tingle beneath my underwear, becoming anxious. He adjusted his position on the couch so he could lick and suck on my breasts. I moaned. I reached behind my own back in order to unzip and remove my skirt and panties. I kicked the leftover clothing to the floor. Naked, I straddled him and sat up, erect. He too was erect—I could nicely feel it between my legs through his jeans.

"Now you have to get naked too," I demanded softly.

Without a word, he quickly complied. Once he was comfortably settled on his back again, I repositioned myself, his huge cock still between my legs but not yet inside. I loved his cock even though it scared me sometimes. It was large—both long and wide. And it curved slightly upwards, much like the curve in a banana. He was cut, but the head of his penis still sat upon a great deal of skin, which made any sort of motion around it smooth and satisfactory. I kissed his neck, his shoulder, his chest. I slid my tongue from one nipple to the other, then down the center of his stomach and toyed with his belly button. Without rushing or stalling, I continued to the edge of his pubic hair, circled around the base of his cock, then down to his balls. I used my tongue to place one nut gently in my mouth. It didn't quite fit, so I sucked on it. Then the other. I never stopped, never ceased my smooth motions. I continued upward, along the underside of his dick. When I reached the head, I circled the entire area, then sucked hard in order to vacuum him into my mouth. I never liked using my hands until I had found a comfortable and pleasurable motion that I could maintain. The task for me was much like tying the stem of a cherry into a knot with my tongue. His cock jumped in my mouth. He moaned, he sighed, he called me "baby." I sucked hard, making sure to keep my mouth extra-wet by not swallowing any saliva that developed. Then I brought in my hands. One hand jerked him off while preventing him from pushing to deep into my throat. The other hand massaged his nuts as if they were a set of Chinese meditation balls.

"Deeper," he grunted, "Take it all the way, baby."

Once again, I obeyed. I held my breath and closed my eyes as I took his cock all the way into my throat. This had always been hard for me to do as I still had my tonsils and tended to gag easy. But for him, I took it—I sucked it up.

"That's a good girl." He liked the way I worked.

He stopped me before he came and instructed me to get a condom. I did so and gently fitted it onto his cock. I climbed back on top of him and forced him inside of me. Once positioned, I slowly sat on it, letting it slip all the way in. I began grinding him, one hand on the back of the couch to keep my balance, the other playing with myself. He responded with hip and hand games. We danced together. He sat up, flipped me over the arm of the couch, and continued fucking me from behind. He grabbed my hair and rode me like a horse. He put his hand around my neck, my mouth, my eyes. Harder. Faster. Rougher.

"I'm gonna come," he moaned. He repeated my name over and over. He gasped, he groaned, he grunted. Suddenly, he pulled out, ripped the condom off, and came all over my back. I felt some of his liquid fly past my ear. Some landed in my hair. But I didn't mind. I let him do anything to me, even if I didn't want it. I took it all, because I wanted him. And I wanted him to want me.

I met my pimp during a relapse—a weekend of alcohol, marijuana, ecstasy and cocaine. I had been having a drug-induced sexual fling with another so-called friend. My pimp happened to be his drug dealer of choice. When we ran dry, we trekked to my pimp's apartment with a handful of cash that I had just retrieved from a nearby ATM. When I first met my pimp, I felt skeptical. He was a large, muscular Cuban from Queens. His arms were covered in tattoos. He wore a wife-beater and baggy jeans that sat too low on his hips. As soon as he opened his mouth, I could tell he had grown up on the streets. I learned he had spent most of his life in prison and was prohibited from leaving the United States. I always had a thing for bad boys.

My pimp and the so-called friend shot the shit for a while after making the transaction. I popped the pills and anxiously waited for them to kick in. The boys discussed prison life and banging pussy—things I couldn't relate to. But once the ecstasy kicked in, I became determined to enter the conversation.

I tended to shift personalities when I felt neglected, especially when I was high. That night, the "street" in me emerged. My dialect and body movements changed. I arched my back to create the illusion of an ass. I pressed my tits together in order to develop some fullness. This turned my pimp on. He warmed up to me. He complimented me by stating that I was "gangsta," a comment which made me blush. Quickly, the so-called friend was the odd man out and I had successfully gained the attention I desired.

After some small talk, we remembered that our meeting was simply for business. The so-called friend and I said good night and excused ourselves. I paused at the front door when my pimp asked for my number. Without hesitation, I gave it to him. And so began my new addiction.

My pimp called several times before I finally responded and paid him a visit. He welcomed me warmly and offered me a soda. For some reason I felt nervous, uncomfortable. I sat several feet away from him on the couch and childishly crossed my legs. I waited for him to make all the moves. We quickly opened up to each other, discussing where we were from and where we had been. We shared our fuck-ups, our break-ups, our toughen-ups. Maybe it was because he seemed so unique. Or maybe it was because he was so different from me. Whatever it was, I immediately developed a dangerous school girl crush.

After an hour or so of casual conversation, something strange came over me. Without thinking and without sugar-coating, I took hold of the discussion and abruptly changed the subject.

"So, do you do anything else?" I asked.

"Other than what?" He responded cautiously.

"Other than deal drugs."

"Such as?"

"I don't know. I mean, like, do you ever sell pussy?"

There was a definite uncomfortable silence. The energy in the room slipped to below zero. He became uncomfortable, agitated, angry.

"Now why the fuck would ask me something like that?"

"I don't know," I desperately tried to cover the hole I had dug for myself.

"Nobody asks a question like that without a reason."

"I'm sorry, I wasn't thinking. Never mind."

Another uncomfortable pause. He stood and began pacing around the room. He nervously rubbed his hand across his smoothly shaved head and took some deep breaths. I watched him contemplate my question. I watched him choose to calm down and come at me more gently.

"I didn't mean to bark at you," he began again. "But I mean it when I say nobody would ask something like that just for no reason."

"I know, I'm sorry," I remained submissive. "I mean, I guess, I really hate my job and I'm looking for something else right now, but I guess I'm also looking to make some extra cash on the side, you know, to help me pay the rent and all."

"Okay. So you're lookin' to sell pussy."

"I don't know. I mean, I've never done it before. I guess I've had sex to get drugs before when the come-down was just too much, but I've never actually, you know, like whored it out or anything."

"So why'd you ask me."

"I guess I just get good vibes off you. I mean, I feel like I can trust you and I feel safe in your company." I was being perfectly honest.

"Well, I'm not gonna lie," he continued slowly. "I feel the same way about you. I mean, with the good vibes and shit."

He gave me nothing to respond to, so I kept quiet. His demeanor changed. He slowed his pacing, thinking intensely to himself, occasionally nodding. I could see the business man in him coming back out.

"I don't like pimps," he finally expressed aloud. "So no, I don't sell pussy. I never have before, but I've never really thought about it."

Silence.

"But there's good money there," he continued. "There's really good money. So, if we were to start somethin' up together, we could get some dough. But I wouldn't be your pimp. I could make arrangements and stick around in case any shit went down, but you'd keep most of the profits. I could just take a small percentage for my services and increase that percentage by selling your customers my drugs."

He continued sharing ideas off the top of his head, almost talking to himself. I nodded in agreement to most of it, only throwing in a comment or question here and there.

"So, are you good?" He asked.

"I'm sorry?" I replied.

"Are you good? Do you give good head. That's what eighty percent of the business would be, you know? Blow jobs. So are you good?"

"Yeah," I almost sounded offended. Of course I'm good. "Of course I'm good. I mean, I get compliments all the time. In fact, I don't think I've ever not gotten a really good review."

From there, we discussed the idea as if I had never offended him to begin with. We exchanged our individual thoughts on rates and services, locations and clients, rules and regulations. When we disagreed, we debated until we could come to a compromise. We cracked jokes about bad ideas and complimented each other on good ones. By the end of it, we had verbally created a blueprint for our new relationship as business partners.

And so began my second new addiction. The first was him—my pimp. The second was getting fucked and sucking dick for money.

Our business ideas grew thin after a while and we decided that the meeting should be adjourned. But he continued to pace nervously.

"What's wrong?" I asked.

"Nothin'. I'm just trying to keep myself professional here."

I laughed. I knew what he meant. He was trying not to fuck me. For a moment I believed that had been my plan all along. Perhaps it had been, on some unconscious level. The silence expanded.

"So," I interrupted, "What's up?"

He stopped pacing. He rubbed his head again and fumbled with the large wad of cash in his pocket. He opened his mouth but nothing came out at first. He stuttered. Finally he stated boldly, "I want you to suck my dick."

My nipples hardened. My pussy tingled.

"Okay," I agreed calmly.

"I want to know for sure whether or not you're any good," he justified.

"I'm down."

The pacing started up again. I was becoming impatient. He stopped.

"How much would you charge me to fuck you?" he finally asked.

"I don't know, um, a hundred bucks?"

"I won't do that," he argued. He retreated to the kitchen and I heard the refrigerator door open and close. He returned with a Ziploc bag containing round, purple pills. He reached inside the bag, grabbed a few, and placed them on the table in front of me. "I'll give you four pills," he continued, "Now how much would you charge me."

I did the math in my head. Each pill was worth fifteen bucks. That's sixty. I bargained with, "Fine. I'll take the four pills, plus twenty bucks for gas and cigarettes."

"Deal."

My pimp returned to the couch and unzipped his jeans. He opened the hole in his boxers and pulled out his dick. He stroked it a little first, but I could tell it was already a bit hard. I kneeled between his legs and dived right in. I teased him a little with my tongue first, then engulfed his cock in my mouth. I sucked hard and fast. I was determined to prove my skill. I was determined to make him come fast. My jaw became cramped. I let him bump into the back of my throat. I jerked him off with my hand, alternating when one began to stiffen up. My eyes began to water. I sucked even harder. Occasionally I'd slow down and give him some gentle, sensual motions, which he obviously liked. This also allowed me to catch my breath and readjust. I'd do both quickly so I could return to the hard, fast sucking. I could tell that was what he liked best. His heavy breathing transformed into low moans. His low moans became "Oh yeah's" and "That's good's." His pelvis gyrated with me. His legs began to twitch. His fists tightened. He was going to come.

His seed filled my mouth and overflowed back onto him. I held the warm, salty liquid in my mouth, looked him in the eye, and swallowed. He liked that too.

He only needed a minute or two before he was ready to go again. We fucked in several positions—me on top, me on the bottom, from behind, standing, upside-down. He was a good fuck. Of course, so was I. I made him come two more times. He got one hell of a good deal for four pills and a twenty. However, it was me who got the upper hand in the end.

"You're amazing," he whispered.

"Thank you." That's all I could say, and I meant it. "So, why don't we both think about this—the ideas we discussed. We can sleep on it then get back to one another later this weekend."

"Alright, baby."

I left his place that afternoon with my third new addiction—his cock.

I started off slow. I was still working full-time at a "normal person's" job for corporate America and only made myself available for the additional work on Friday and Saturday nights. But I was pleased with the extra one to

three hundred dollars in my pocket per week. My pimp
made all the arrangements for my first few dates. Eventually,
I began finding my own business. During this time, he was
the only man I regularly fucked for no pay. My crush on him
only heightened, even though in retrospect he was simply
using me for the extra cash. I began to place him on a
throne, doing anything he asked. I'd even bring him dinner
or run to the store and buy him cigarettes. I had never been
a submissive woman outside of the bedroom before. For
some reason, it was different with him.

For a while, every time I went to my pimp's place to hang
out, a job or two eventually came before the night was over.
After the first month or so, less and less clients were
appearing there and more were requesting in-call dates.
Sometimes I would meet a man in the office or in my car, if
the price was right. It also depended on the client and how
important my anonymity was with that particular individual.
My regular clients knew my real name, but the dates my
pimp arranged did not. My pimp and I both became stressed
over our "other jobs," which had caused some moodiness
and tension when we were in each other's presence. That
tension quickly increased over time.

It was a Wednesday night. I had been invited to a dinner
for my day job. My pimp and I had already agreed to try to
get some work that night, but I had plenty of time to grub
first. We decided that he would simply call once he knew all
the details. It was late before I realized that my phone had
died. I rushed to my car, started the engine, and plugged my
cell phone into my car charger. I had missed six calls from
my pimp. He had left a couple voice mails and sent several
text messages.

I listened to the voice mails first, "Call me ASAP,"
followed by, "What the fuck is wrong with you? Call me
now!"

The text messages were all the same—Are we gonna get this dough or what?

I called him immediately. Thanks to caller ID, I was greeted with, "Where the hell are you!"

He was angry, I was drunk.

"I'm sorry," I pleaded. "I had a dinner with management tonight and we had some drinks afterward."

"Is that so?" He obviously didn't believe me. He always assumed I was getting high or fucking off.

"Yes!"

"I had a large group of guys over here about an hour ago. They were interested. And now they're gone. Get over here. I might still be able to get you some work."

Then he hung up.

My eyes filled with tears. I sped to my pimp's apartment, fully aware of my flawed driving capabilities. When the front door opened, instead of letting me in, he directed me out.

"We're going somewhere," he announced.

Normally, I would have asked where. But in that moment, I didn't dare.

We returned to my car and I followed his every direction. Our destination was the bare apartment of two young Japanese men, who were celebrating their final night in the states before returning home. At $150 apiece for a half hour each individually, plus the protection of my pimp, I felt it was a fair deal and was grateful for the work. My goal for the evening was to finish each client as quickly as possible, long before their time was up. My pimp waited in the living room with one of the guys while I joined the other in his bedroom. The first man was not much thicker than me and only a few inches taller. He seemed sweet, shy, slightly embarrassed. He was drowning in his plain white undershirt and sweat pants.

Tonight's gonna be easy, I thought to myself, giving him a quick look over.

I started how I tended to start most of my full-service dates, by standing on my tip-toes, wrapping my arms around his neck, and slowly sucking on his ear. He laughed from the tickling sensation then pressed his lips against mine. His tongue felt warm yet naïve in my mouth. There was definitely something sweet and innocent about him that allowed me to fully loosen up. The alcohol still flowing through my body added some extra reassurance.

"Do you wanna lay on the bed?" I asked meekly.

"Uh huh," he mumbled. I could hear his thick, broken English, even when he spoke in noises rather than words.

I led him to his futon mattress against the wall then lay on my back with my legs spread wide. Like I said, I wanted to keep this date quick and easy.

He laughed again. "I'm sorry, I've never done this before," he apologized.

"Never paid for it, or never had sex?" I inquired.

"Neither."

Ooh, a virgin. Suddenly, the act I usually had to be high or drunk to successfully do seemed extremely easy.

We fucked in silence. But I couldn't call it a "fuck." It definitely wasn't "making love" either, something I admittedly had never done before anyway. We simply—slept together—sweet and gentle, much like two young high school kids mutually agreeing to try it together for the first time. I felt like I was losing my virginity all over again.

He came quick, but not so quick that I was left unsatisfied. I was again reminded of how it was never about the money for me—it had always been about the sex and the power.

We exited the bedroom with about ten minutes to spare.

"Done already?" my pimp eyed me suspiciously.

"Yep," I replied without making eye contact.

He approached me, gently touched my arm and whispered in my ear, "Good girl."

I smiled. "I'll be in the bedroom, then."

I casually laid back down on the futon and patiently waited for my next client. The second man entered momentarily and walked toward me shyly. He was larger than the first man, slightly overweight. But he had a much younger demeanor about himself. His face was round and still contained most of its baby fat. He seemed even more gentle and innocent than the first.

"Hi," I purred.

"Hi." He too spoke in thick, broken English, though more soft-spoken. "I'm sorry, I'm nervous."

These two must spend a lot of time together, I thought, noting how similar their words were.

He laid next to me on the futon, unable to make the first move. I caressed his hair, his face, his chest. I quickly moved down to his genitals where he was already hard and toyed with it through his pants. I slipped my hand under the elastic of his sweats and into his boxers. I stroked it. I teased it. I briefly removed my hand in order to spit on my palm then returned to my duty. His breathing became heavy. He moaned. He came.

Nice.

"Oh my God," he grunted. "I'm sorry, I came so fast."

"It's okay," I consoled sweetly. "I like that."

"I'm sorry," he continued apologizing over and over.

"No, please don't apologize. Really, it's okay."

Once again I felt like we were both virgins, and perhaps he was. The only difference between him and his friend was that he would remain a virgin even after my services. I allowed him to cuddle with me for a while. We chatted about Japan and where he was from. Why he was going back, why he was in America to begin with. We chatted like two kids on their first date. It was great.

This time when I exited the bathroom, my pimp was even more impressed. He touched my hair and caressed my cheek. For a moment, I felt like he was my father, praising me after I had won a grade school spelling bee.

We said our good-byes to the two boys, exited the apartment, and walked back to my car. My pimp counted the cash in his hand and gave me $260. The rest covered his fee for arranging the job and for standing by.

"The second guy came from a hand job only," I bragged.

"That's my girl," he smiled.

I blushed. We continued walking in silence. The memory of him yelling at me and treating me like a little girl earlier that night disappeared instantly. My first addiction increased dramatically. I felt butterflies in my stomach, which I immediately mistook for falling in love. I kept that belief for weeks, only finding the maturity to conclude them as false after my heart had been severely broken.

When the amount of work increased, but my availability did not, my pimp expressed new ideas of finding more willing girls to join us and begin a sort of "real" escort service. I was into it and worked hard to find those girls. I did everything from posting ads on Craigslist to picking up girls at bars, to starting casual conversations with women while standing in line at the post office. I refused to disappoint him.

The first and only girl I actually brought to him was a young, meth-addict whom I had met while she temped at my day job. She was attractive, dark and pierced. I found her to be the perfect candidate once we freely began discussing our sex and drug habits. We hung out during our lunch breaks for several days before I finally called her on a whim and invited her to meet my pimp. I had already shared the possible idea of her joining our clique prior to that night and knew it was going to be a success.

She and my pimp hit it off immediately. I smiled proudly as the two of them discussed their lives, their goals, their interests. We drank Jack and Coke and shared a dank blunt. We refrained from discussing business, as my pimp and the girl had already spoken over the phone regarding logistics.

The Jack stirred the pills and cocaine already inside my body from earlier that evening. The room began to spin. I did not feel sick, simply lost and excessively sociable. I chatted with the girl non-stop, and downloaded music from the internet and played her my favorite songs. I caressed her hair and rubbed her shoulders. Though I was disoriented and could no longer make out the details in her face, I could feel that she was beautiful.

The three of us retreated to the bedroom to make ourselves more comfortable. We laid together, her head in my lap, my head in his. We listened to music and slipped into euphoria. I eventually excused myself to the use the restroom. When I sat on the toilet seat, I flipped on the tiny wall heater by my feet. The warmth caused a sensation I had never experienced before. It burned my toes and traveled up to my knees, then my thighs, then my crotch. The subtle air between my legs made me drip, even long after I had emptied my bladder.

When I returned, the girl was laying her head in my pimp's lap. He was gently massaging her head, her shoulders, her breasts. A sudden twinge of jealousy swept through my body. The drugs and alcohol assisted in turning that jealousy into anger. But I refused to show it. I sat at the foot of the bed and joined them. I rubbed her feet and she moaned in satisfaction.

Eventually, my pimp excused himself to take a phone call in the other room. When he left, I asked the girl if she wanted to get high with me, maybe take some ecstasy. Though I could tell she was craving crystal more than anything, she agreed. Then I leaned into her and made my first major mistake.

"If you want to fuck him," I stated, "That's okay, just make sure to get something from him."

"What do you mean?" she asked.

"I mean, I don't mind, but set a price, like a couple of pills for us both or something."

She was blatantly offended. But like me, she tried hard not to show it.

"Never mind," I continued. "I'm outta cash tonight, but I'll try to get more from him."

I exited the bedroom to converse with my pimp out in the hallway. He seemed agitated from the phone conversation he had just ended.

"Hey," I started gingerly, "She wants a pill but she doesn't have any money. But she said she'll give you anything else you might want."

He too, was blatantly offended. I knew immediately that I had made my second mistake of the night.

"Whaddya mean, 'anything else I might want?'" he growled.

"I don't know," I lied.

"Wait here."

He stormed back into the bedroom and slammed the door behind him. I could hear him speaking, but I couldn't make out the words. Every so often, the girl would try to respond, but I could tell he wasn't letting her. I knew I had been caught in my childish game. I waited in the living room, smoking a cigarette. After a while, my pimp came out of the bedroom and stormed toward me.

"She told me she has no idea what you're talking about!" he yelled.

I couldn't respond.

"And now," he continued, "she's sitting in my bedroom crying because I just went off at her, apparently for no reason! So who's tellin' the truth here?"

"I'm sorry," I finally pleaded, "It's my fault. I don't know, I'm not thinking clearly. I think there was a misunderstanding."

"You're damn right there was a misunderstanding! But here's the real problem; she doesn't know what the fuck is going on and now she doesn't trust either one of us. You may have just ruined our chances of doing business with her."

I nodded, keeping my eyes to the ground. By then, I was in tears, unable to justify any of my actions, and knowing it.

"Stay out here until you've got your head back on straight," he demanded. "And don't come asking me for nothin'!"

He stormed out of the living room and returned to the bedroom. I buried my head in my hands and cried. The drama had forced some of the intoxication out of me. I quickly began to sober up and attempted to retrace what had happened throughout the night. All I could decipher was that suddenly I was the bad guy.

I dozed off on the couch and woke to find that nearly an hour had passed. I was alone. I slowly got to my feet, my head pounding. I wasn't sure if anyone was even still home, so I decided to retrieve my purse and jacket out of the bedroom and leave. As I made my way down the hallway, I could hear music quietly playing through the bedroom door. I knocked.

"Who is it!" my pimp's voice bounced against the walls.

"It's me," I replied

"Come in."

I did as I was told. When I entered the bedroom, I found my pimp and the girl lying in his bed together. They were under the covers but I could tell they were naked. The room smelled of sex. A blade sliced into my heart. I held back the tears.

"I'm gonna head out," I mumbled.

I grabbed my purse and jacket, which were lying on the floor next to the closet. I moved slowly, as if to give him more time to ask me to stay. But he didn't. I exited, and just as I was about to shut the door behind me, my pimp made one final demand.

"You need to learn to think before you talk."

And with that, I left.

Everything was ruined and I knew it. I knew that I had gotten myself into a situation I didn't deserve to be in. Yes, I had fucked up, but I also did not deserve to be treated like a little girl. I was angry. No, I was fucking pissed off. During the drive home, I had to slap myself several times to stop the tears so I could watch the road. I spent the rest of the weekend in bed trying to cry myself to sleep, but the memory of his words and my actions kept me awake. I frantically searched my apartment for a blade, but only dug up dirty butter knives and a pair of scissors, the kind for cutting hair. Weighing my options, I grabbed the scissors and pressed one of the blades hard against my wrist. When I sliced through my skin, the blood came fast and poured onto my black bed sheets. I sucked on the wound, finding comfort in the taste of my own blood. Cutting was like a drug to me. Finally, I was able to fall asleep.

After that one night, I promised myself that I would never see or talk to my pimp again. I knew I was at fault for the negative outcome of that evening, but I still believed I had been unnecessarily disrespected. My pimp called and I successfully ignored it, though it was extremely difficult to do so. Of course, because my pimp also served as my drug dealer at that time, I was eventually forced to give in.

"Are you stocked?" I asked him over the phone.

"What color?" he rushed.

"Purple or blue, I guess."

"Oh, those. I've got red ones."

"Fine. I'll be there in about twenty minutes."

I had just wrapped up another stressful day at work and had been sober for nearly three days. I was in desperate need of a pick-up and had cut off all the other drug dealers and users I knew. He was my only source.

I pulled into the driveway and parked my car. My boots made a loud, repetitive clunk with each step I took toward his apartment. I knocked.

"Who!?"

"It's me."

Soon, I heard the locks being turned and I was invited in. As usual, my pimp looked pissed off. I still hadn't gotten used to his total lack of hospitality.

"I'll get four," I started, handing him a few bills.

He grabbed the money, exited to his bedroom, and returned with four tiny red pills, each with two small cherries etched on the top. I popped two of the pills immediately and saved the rest for later.

"Thanks," I muttered. "I guess I'll talk to you later."

"Okay."

As my hand touched the knob of the front door, he stopped me.

"Hey!" he shouted, probably not meaning to. "What are you doin' tonight?"

"Nothin'. Just going home."

"Why don't you hang around here for a bit. There might be some work later tonight and I want to discuss some things with you."

"Okay." A part of me wanted to say "no," but I agreed without hesitation.

We sat on the living room couch together watching bad stand-up comedy on television. Finally it was him who broke the uncomfortable silence.

"You really fucked up the other night, you know."

"I know."

"I tried calling you."

"I know."

"Well, why didn't you answer?"

"I was asleep, I guess."

"Well, you fucked up again. We coulda made some good money the other night, and instead, we got nothin' cause you felt like sleeping!"

"Sorry." I shifted my eyes to the floor.

We both focused our attention back on the television.

"I don't know what's the matter with you, and I don't really care," he started again, "But are we gonna still do this or not?"

"Yeah, of course." Then back to the floor, then to the television, then the floor again. Nearly twenty minutes passed in complete silence.

"C'mon, then." He said. "Let's go to my room."

I obediently followed him. His room smelled dank from a recently smoked blunt. I was grateful the scent of sex had deteriorated. He sat in front of his laptop and searched for an MP3 to play. I placed my purse and jacket at their usual location on the floor and remained standing by the door.

"Sit down," he said as sweetly as he could. "Make yourself comfortable."

I obeyed. I started to removed my boots, but quickly changed my mind.

"Go ahead, take off your shoes."

"My feet are cold," I replied.

My pimp casually adjusted himself so that he sat behind me. I could feel his warm love-handles rub against my own. He placed his hands on my shoulders and began to massage my upper back.

"Did you miss me?" he asked.

"A little bit."

He laughed, "I guess that's all I deserve, huh? A little bit."

I smiled.

"You know, I care about you and I don't mean to treat you shitty," he continued. "That other night, when you left here, it tore my heart apart."

And in that moment, I fell in love with him all over again.

"Why don't you take off your clothes?" he asked. It was the first time he had ever asked me to do something rather than demand it.

Once again, I did as I was told. I removed my boots first, unzipping them slowly one at a time. Then I removed my tank top and bra. My nipples were already hard from the cold. I slowly unzipped my pants and slid them off, finally followed by my socks and underwear. My pimp had stripped down to his boxers and usual white wife beater. Unexpectedly, he grabbed my chin and shoved his tongue into my mouth. We had never kissed on the lips before. He tasted sweet and salty at the same time. He pinched my nipples, then licked them, then bit them. I was already soaking wet. I kept my hands to myself, unsure of what he wanted. He pushed me onto my back and aggressively opened my legs. Without warning, he buried his face in my crotch. He had never eaten me out before either. In fact, he had, more than once, made it very clear that he never would. But that night, he licked and sucked my pussy as if his life depended on it. He maneuvered the lips of my vagina with his finger tips in order to lick every crevice he could find. He teased my clit—licking it fast and hard, then slow and gentle, then fast again, then suddenly pulled away and shoved his tongue inside of me. I felt my juices overflow and lubricate my asshole. My pimp noticed and took it as his opportunity to help open me up. He inserted first one finger in my ass, then eventually another. He continued eating me out— hungrily, as if he were a stray dog who had found leftovers in an easily accessible trash can.

"Oh, baby," I moaned, "You treat me so good."

And I came.

Pleased with his work, he immediately removed his clothing and stretched out on his back. I knew that was my cue. I started the same way as usual because I knew that was what he wanted. I teased the area around his cock, occasionally touching his skin, but primarily letting my warm breath flow through his pubic hair. I used only the extreme tip of my tongue to gently lick his balls. Then, with my hands behind my back, I took him into my mouth, sucking hard but slow. I took him in deep—deep enough to feel the head of his dick bypass my tonsils, nearly causing me to gag. I struggled to pull back in order to catch my breath. I spit, lubricating him with my saliva. I swallowed his bitter pre-cum and inhaled his masculine scent. I heard the crinkle of a condom wrapper being fumbled with then thrown on the floor. I pulled my head away from his lap so he could unroll the rubber onto his dick.

"Come here," he whispered.

I crawled on top of him and straddled his cock. I rubbed my crotch against his to coat the condom with my wetness. I used my hand to position him, then slowly sat down, taking him all the way in. We moaned together. We moved together. I angled myself in different ways by first placing my hands on his chest, then on the wall behind him, then on my own hips. The muscles in my thighs began to burn. He grabbed my waist and helped guide my hard, fast movements up and down, then forward and backward. He grabbed my ass with both hands and lifted me as he sat up. He forced me under him, on my back, and took the lead. He fucked me hard. With every thrust, his cock hit something inside of me, forcing me to grunt, forcing me to cry out in pain. But I took it. The pain only made me wetter, made me want more. He placed my ankles on his shoulders while he fucked me. Then he pushed my legs over my head until the tops of my feet touched the comforter above me. Then he closed my legs and shoved them to one side. With every contortion he put me in, he never once broke his rhythm. He shoved his finger into my mouth and I sucked on it. Then he used my saliva to lubricate my asshole. He briefly teased that area then slowly inserted his finger back inside of me. He flipped me onto my hands and knees without pulling out. My body rotated around his dick the way a ham slowly spins in an oven. It wasn't until I had situated myself, elbows on the bed and ass in the air, when he finally came to a stop. When he pulled out, I felt my juices drip down the insides of my thighs. He put his fingers inside of me to catch the liquid, and then moved back to my asshole. He removed the condom then repositioned himself. The first time he entered my ass, it hurt so much I automatically pulled away. It only took a second attempt for me to discover the best way to angle myself so I could take his dick all the way in. His grunts and moans turned into "Fuck yeahs" and "Oh shits." My asshole opened wide to swallow him whole and became slick from the mixture of both of our juices. His thrusts became faster and harder until I could no longer support myself on my knees and elbows. I laid flat on my stomach and left him to do the work on top of me. I could feel his sweaty chest pressed against my back. Our heads fell next to each other, cheek to cheek. I craned my neck so I could kiss him. Our tongues danced in our mouths. We swallowed each other, never pulling away.

"Turn over!" he gasped, suddenly pulling out.

I did as I was told. His stream of cum hit my chin first, then my ear, and finally my lips and tongue. I opened my mouth wide to catch as much of it as I could. It had never tasted so sweet or felt so hot before. I drank as much as I could, needing to swallow twice to get it all down. Then we both collapsed on the bed, utterly exhausted. For several minutes, the only sounds we heard were our heavy gasps for air and the passing of cars outside. Finally, we simultaneously sat up—me for some water and him for a cigarette.

"Fuck, I needed that," he admitted.

I smiled, cuddled up next to him, and fell asleep in his arms.

I was awoken in the middle of the night by the sound of a steady beep coming from his computer. I looked up to find that someone was trying to instant message him. The picture of the sender consisted of a dark, slender woman sitting with her legs spread wide, fingering herself. The message read, Hey, big boy. Whatcha doin'? Intrigued, I sat up and placed my hands on the keyboard. Nothin'. Wut about you? I pressed enter and waited. Almost immediately, another message popped up. Thinkin' bout your big dick.

"What the fuck are you doing!"

I quickly turned around to find my pimp staring at me, eyes blaring.

"Nothing," I replied meekly. "Just typing a message."

"To who?!"

"I don't know."

He sat up and leaned in closer so he could see the screen. His face reddened when he saw his user name in the messaging window.

"Who the fuck do you think you are!" he screamed. "What is so fucked up about you that you think it's alright to touch my shit?"

"I'm sorry," I stuttered. "It just popped up. I only typed one thing."

"Bullshit! I wake up to find you chatting on my computer and pretending to be me!"

"You're overreacting," I argued.

"Shut the fuck up!!!"

I did. By then I was in tears.

"I don't know what's wrong with you," he continued, slightly calmer. "But I'm starting to think we're gonna have to cut ties and go our separate ways."

I tried to read his eyes through my blurred vision. They didn't waiver. I slowly stood up to find that my hands and legs were shaking. I struggled to get dressed and collect my things. I walked out of his bedroom, out of his apartment, and out of his life.

I swore never to go back. I swore never to talk to him again. I swore to delete his number from my phone and move on with my life. The rest of that weekend I locked myself inside my apartment, lied in bed and cried. I called in sick to work on Monday. I finally sat up and pondered what to do next. My head was throbbing, so I grabbed a bottled of extra strength Tylenol from the cabinet in my bathroom. I popped two pills then waited. I was starting to experience withdrawals from my usual cocaine or ecstasy or Xanax. So I popped two more. My headache slowly weakened, but the hot-cold flashes and severe shaking would not. So I popped two, then three, then two more. The room began to spin. I was up to eleven, then twelve, then fourteen, then twenty-one . . .

When I saw my pimp again, I had completed a month of rehabilitation and had a significant amount of clean time under my belt. I held him tightly and inhaled his memorable scent. I told him that I wouldn't be coming around anymore—that a recovering drug addict couldn't continue seeing her drug dealer. He asked me if I was going to fuck him. When I said "no," he promptly flipped open his phone and made other plans for the night. When I told him good bye, he asked me to call his cell so he would have my new number. I told him I would. I lied.

The Predator

She was hungry. She hadn't eaten in nearly a month and was desperately drooling. She throbbed uncontrollably at the thought of being fed. I spread my legs wider in order to stretch her anxious jaws. She thanked me by pulsating harder then continued to wait for her prey. When it entered her mouth, she swallowed it whole. She salivated frantically, never ceasing to rest or inhale anything but it. She chewed and sucked, savoring every bit of flavor. When it tried to pull out in order to readjust, she clamped around it tightly, refusing to let her meal get away. She sucked harder and faster, forcing it to give her what she wanted—the sweetest part of her food—the warm, liquid interior, which could only be extracted shortly before its death. She swallowed its exhaust in one swift gulp, then finally relaxed—satisfied. I left my legs spread in order to allow her to release the leftover bones and non-chewable fat. It pulled out and I wiped her mouth with my t-shirt. She inhaled deeply, slowly released the air, and then promptly fell asleep.

I had spent three weeks satisfying my sexual urges with nothing except my right hand. The days often passed slowly, especially when I didn't have any scheduled obligations except attending drug and alcohol treatment in the evening. It was a Monday night. The small, informal group of recovering addicts that I met with shared their addictions, their anxiety and their amends. After a brief smoke break, we returned to the recreation room where we met. Several people joined us late—a couple of regulars and one man I had never seen before. He must have been in his late-twenties. He wore his moustache and short beard extremely well. His tall body was dressed in a t-shirt advertising a local tattoo parlor, and tan khakis with a long chain secured to the belt loop. I looked him over once and liked what I saw. When the meeting resumed, we both started to speak at the same time. I blushed and gestured for him to go ahead. He politely thanked me and introduced himself to the group.

"Hi. I'm Blake," he began. "This is my first time coming here."

The group welcomed him with warm smiles.

"I'm from Chicago," he continued, "And I'm here to get treatment for cocaine addiction."

Ah, I thought. Already we have something in common.

He briefly shared the details of his addiction then concluded with, "Thanks for having me."

Again, the group welcomed him then waited patiently for the next volunteer to speak. I took the opportunity and introduced myself.

"It's funny," I started. "When I was using, any news was bad news, or I'd get worked up over the littlest things. But now, I understand that everything happens for a reason, and that realization helps me get through the day much easier."

There were nods of agreement from several people.

"This morning, I had to go in for a biopsy," I continued. "They're not sure what the problem is, I'll get the lab results in about a week. Back in the day, I probably would have gotten stressed about it, but today I just kind of laughed and told myself, 'Well, that's what you get when you have a lot of unprotected sex.'"

Again, nods of agreement. I glanced at Blake to make sure I had caught his interest. By the concerned look on his face, I figured I had.

"When I got home, I found out that a short erotic story I had written was accepted for publication in an online magazine. I told my mom and she asked me what kind of story it was and I just sort of giggled. Then she was like, 'Oh, that kind story. That good. It better you write sex than have sex.'"

The group laughed at my weak attempt to imitate my mother's broken English.

"I guess it's just funny to me how my addiction to sex came up in two totally different contexts today, and really the only one I'm still thinking about is the one that makes me laugh. Thanks, that's it."

The others thanked me and the meeting continued. I rose to serve myself more coffee.

"I was wondering if there was coffee."

I turned to find Blake behind me, preparing a cup for himself.

"Oh yeah," I replied, "We've got to be addicted to something."

He laughed. I reached for the coffee pot, but his hand stopped me. He took the pot from me and poured me a cup.

She's always had a mind of her own. And she's vindictive and unmerciful. She captures prisoners, tortures them, and then throws them back into the world without a dime or clothes on their backs. She often did things that I didn't approve of. Sometimes she'd eat things that would make me sick, and no matter how much I protested, she'd do it again.

I had decided to remain celibate for the entirety of my month-long treatment. Over the past several years, I had not only developed an addiction to drugs, but one to sex as well. As they say, it's not what you're addicted to, it's the fact that you have the disease of addiction.

When Blake's hand brushed against mine, I felt her squirm beneath me. Her eyes opened. Her ears perked up.

Down, girl, I thought. But like usual, she never listened.

The meeting the following night started off unusually slow. My anxiety level was painfully high and prevented me from sitting still. The half a dozen cups of coffee I had already devoured probably didn't help either, but I proceeded to refill my serving anyway.

"Getting your fix, huh?" Blake wrapped his arm around my waist and whispered into my ear.

"You know it," I replied.

I reached for the sugar but found the dispenser to be empty. I looked around for more but to no avail. I shot Blake a disappointed look then returned to my seat. I impatiently listened to other members of the group speak. I had nothing to say that night and didn't feel much like listening either. My complete lack of attention was interrupted by a gentle tap on my shoulder. I turned to find Blake and was greeted with a seemingly empty coffee cup. I took it from him and peeked inside—sugar.

"Where'd you get this?" I whispered.

"The kitchen," he replied.

Who woulda thunk?

"Thanks."

For the remainder of the meeting, I occasionally turned my head to smile at Blake. He always smiled back. I had to struggle to prevent myself from making any moves right then and there. I wanted to touch him. I wanted to rest my head on his shoulder. I wanted to feel his warm breath against my neck. But I was determined to be good. I was determined to make it the entire month staying abstinent from all my personal addictions.

After the meeting, I sat on the curb outside and lit a cigarette. Other members of the group were doing the same while chatting and saying their good nights. Blake joined me and I couldn't help but rest my thigh against his.

"Nice night," he mumbled.

"Yeah."

My leg was shaking from the anxiety and immense amounts of coffee in my system. He firmly placed his hand on my knee and held it down.

"I know, it's terrible," I laughed.

"I'm sure the coffee didn't help either."

"Nope."

He pulled his hand away. I felt a rush of disappointment flow through my body. It had felt nice there. It would probably feel nice in other places too.

"Shut up," I whispered to myself.

"What?" Blake asked.

"Nothing."

We chatted about where we were from and where we had been. We discussed what had brought us to treatment and what we were planning to do after we had finished. By the end of our conversation, we were the only people left in the parking lot.

"I better get going," I said.

"Yeah, me too."

We stood. I thought about simply walking away and shouting a good night over my shoulder. Unfortunately, that didn't work out.

"Good night," I stood on my toes and wrapped my arms around his neck.

He returned the hug. His hands felt large and masculine around my tiny waist. I didn't want him to let go. But he did, and so did I.

"See you tomorrow night, then?" he asked.

"Absolutely."

I rushed to my car without turning back and quickly drove home.

During the day I am usually able to keep her under control. I was the one that trained her, so I was also the one to keep her in order. However, during the night, she often got away with doing whatever she wanted—especially when I was asleep.

That night, I dreamed of Blake. He was touching me, licking me, eating me. He slapped his cock against my clit and fucked me. In my dreams, sex was always simple and straight-forward, quick and to the point. I woke in the middle of the night with her between my legs, jumping around like a little toddler. I grabbed her tightly to hold her down.

Why do you always have to wake me when I'm having the best dreams? I asked her.

Like usual, her only response was to tickle herself so an unbearable sensation rushed through every vein in my body. That was how she kept me under control. She begged me to touch her. When I failed to comply, she tried a different tactic.

It's okay, she purred. If you touch me, it's not sex. You won't be breaking any rules.

She's right, I thought.

I removed my pajama pants and underwear and neatly folded them at the foot of my bed. I kicked off the covers and opened my legs wide. Hesitantly, I reached between my legs and gently touched her. She was soaking wet—salivating all over herself and dripping down my ass. I touched her harder, pressing against the top of her head then sliding my fingers to the bottoms of her feet. She moaned. I moaned. I moved my hand faster, picking up speed, unable to slow down, unable to stop. It was too late. She had already seduced me and there was no turning back. I forced my finger inside her mouth and she sucked on it viciously. Then I returned to her head, the place she loved being massaged the most. I arched my back and closed my eyes. I licked the fingers on my other hand and slowly teased my nipples. She growled, she roared, she screamed. She sucked, she bit, she swallowed. She took my hand as if it were the last piece of meat on the planet. She inhaled deeper, forcing me to push harder and faster. My legs began to shake. My heavy breathing turned into uncontrollable moans. I pictured Blake in my head. I imagined his naked body and his cock slipping in and out of her. I imagined a pleasure neither she nor I had experienced in weeks. Then she came. I spasmed, my legs and lower back forced to follow her lead. I frantically pulled my hand away. The orgasm was so intense that I begged her to stop. I begged her never to stop. It was if she had binged and could do nothing but vomit her juices onto my sheets. When she finished purifying her stomach, I was kept awake by her heavy breathing. Soon, my breathing became one with hers and together, we fell asleep.

Blake agreed to go out for coffee with me after the meeting the following evening. I paid the barista while he carried the hot mugs.

"Do you want to sit inside or outside?" I asked.

"I like it inside," he replied.

"Me too." Insert dirty joke here. "Insert dirty joke here," I laughed.

He liked my punch line and we continued repeating it whenever we said something that could have been interpreted sexually—which was just about everything.

After we finished our drinks, we walked to the riverfront to enjoy the nonexistent view. We lit each other's cigarettes and smoked together in silence. I laid my head on his thigh.

"Don't tell me to move my head a little to the right," I smiled.

"I wasn't going to."

Again, silence.

"You know," he continued. "We can't get drunk, but we can pretend like we're drunk."

"Was that a really poor attempt at a pick-up line?"

"No! What do you mean?"

"Well, I don't know what you do when you're drunk . . ."

He caught my drift and blushed.

"Anyway, I never make the first move," he argued.

"Me neither."

Silence. I repositioned my body and he gently began to massage my back. I grabbed his thigh firmly—close, but not too close. He slipped his hand under my shirt and continued massaging my lower back. We watched the periodic police cars pass as we continued not making the first move.

"Okay," Blake broke the silent sexual tension, "Now move your head a little to the right."

I laughed and playfully slapped his arm. I rotated onto my back and he began to massage my chest. I could feel his hands wanting to move lower, to grab me, to tease me. I arched my back, forcing his finger tips to accidentally brush against one of my nipples. He acted as if he hadn't noticed and continued his smooth movements.

Minutes seemed to pass like hours. When I couldn't stand the tension any longer, I turned my head toward him and forcefully pressed my lips against his. He responded aggressively. He grabbed my face in his hands and shoved his tongue into my mouth. Without hesitation, he slipped his hands underneath my shirt and bra and squeezed my breasts hard. I wrapped my hand tightly around the crotch of his pants. We moaned together. He started to slip his hand down the front of my jeans, but I stopped him.

"I'm on my period."

"Shit."

But we fucked anyway. I was hungry. I spread my legs wide for him. I was dripping wet and throbbing from undeniable temptation. When he entered me, I swallowed him whole. I squeezed, tightening my opening, savoring every bit of flavor. When he tried to pull out in order to readjust, I clamped around him tightly. I refused to let him go. I refused to let him slow down, not even the headlights of passing cars could distract me. He used one hand to satisfy my clit and the other to play with my breasts. I gyrated my hips, loving everything he did. I moaned each time his cock hit something inside of me. The familiar pain felt good. I didn't want him to stop, but I knew I was ready to come.

"Ladies first," he whispered.

And I let go. The orgasm forced me to lose complete control of my body. My arms, my legs, my torso shook desperately. I screamed out in euphoria when I felt his body do the same. We held each other tightly as we came together. I swallowed him in one swift gulp, then finally relaxed— satisfied. I left my legs spread in order to keep him inside of me for a moment longer. He pulled out and I wiped myself with my t-shirt. We lay together on the cold bench, breathing heavily. I inhaled deeply, rested my head on his chest, then promptly fell asleep.

You made me do it.

She laughed and told me to shut up.

We were lying in bed, contemplating the events of that evening. I felt good. I felt guilty for feeling good. I wondered if I had seduced him or if he had seduced me. Or perhaps it was a mutual agreement. I had had so many one-sided confrontations in my life that I couldn't tell the difference. I reminisced about Blake's cock sliding in and out of me. I wanted to touch myself, but I held back. I wanted more, I wanted it again. I could feel her begging me for another round.

It wasn't me, she argued, as if reading my mind. It was all you. I wasn't even in the mood, not with all the blood I've been spitting up lately.

I couldn't argue back.

Pretty soon, she continued, We won't know who's in control anymore.

And then she was gone.

The Bitch

I don't know why I'm here.

I am surrounded by more people than I can handle. I always become claustrophobic in crowds, whether it's a crowd of twelve or twelve thousand. Actually, I'd prefer twelve thousand. At least then I'd become mostly invisible— a little fish in a big pond, or whatever. I know this. So why do I keep putting myself in these situations? I feel awkward. It's getting difficult to breathe. I don't look nearly as good as the rest of the women here. And everybody is drinking. God, I wish I could have a drink. I'll just give it another twenty minutes. By then, everyone will be drunk and they won't notice if I sneak out. Fuck. This wouldn't be so bad if I had brought a date. I tried, but none of them were interested. Of course, last week they all wanted to see me on the same night. But I already had plans, so I saw none of them. The story of my life.

I hate cast parties. They're just another excuse to get drunk and laid. And it's not like I'm really going to miss any of these people if I never get to see them again. I'm such a bitch. I need a cigarette. Shit. Of course, the smoking clique has already claimed territory outside. Half of these people aren't even smokers. Posers. The worst part about being out here is that the fake smokers are going to bum cigarettes off the real smokers because, despite all the scientific and socially unacceptable disgusting facts we all know about the habit, they still think it will make them cool. Then, not only am I one less cigarette, but I further take the risk of getting my lighter stolen—again. To avoid this inconvenience, I succumb to lighting the fake smoker's cigarette for him, and shift impatiently while he struggles to suck hard enough to get the damn thing going. At the same time, my own cigarette is quickly burning away under the natural process of flame and oxygen, and becoming shorter and shorter, and the nicotine is sucked into the abyss of nothingness when it should be damaging my body so I can get cancer as soon as possible. But it doesn't even end here. Because I watch the fake smoker and it's undeniably apparent that he's not even enjoying the cigarette. In fact, it's so disgusting to him, that he tosses it on the ground and stomps it out before he's even halfway through. And again, half of a cigarette, which I paid for, is wasted.

God, I hate everyone. Now, do I light up another one and remain standing out here in the cold, or do I tip-toe away, get in my car and drive to freedom? Of course, there's probably no need for me to tip-toe because it's highly likely that if I just disappeared nobody would notice. But then I'd have to deal with the wrath of the one or two people who will inevitably approach me tomorrow night with an interrogation of, "Where did you go? What happened to you last night? Why didn't you say goodbye?" These will be the people who noticed I was gone because they wanted to bum another cigarette but they couldn't find me and all the other smokers were either out or only carrying menthols.

I might as well light up another one while I contemplate the pros and cons of leaving versus staying. There's an obnoxious bitch dominating the attention of the smokers-slash-fake-smokers clique. Damn, she's loud. How can anyone be that loud and not want to punch themselves in the face? Or is she just always this loud and therefore, thinks she's being totally normal? Where did she come from anyway? Over half the people here aren't even cast members. They must be the boyfriends and girlfriends and roommates and buddies and pals of cast members. Or maybe of the crew. Probably invited themselves over to network and drink free beer. If I wanted to be surrounded by this type of environment, I would have stayed in college.

Fortunately, through a handful of experiences such as this, I've trained myself to turn down the volume around me. I space out while maintaining eye contact, smiling and nodding, always knowing the correct moments to throw in an indifferent "yeah" or "right." Which is exactly what I do while so-and-so's boyfriend blabs to me about the current production he's understudying for. As if I care. But I can't help slipping continuous glances over at this girl. If I really wanted to get honest, I'd have to say that I think she'd be beautiful if I could just tape her mouth shut.

This is what happens when I don't go to meetings and don't do my step work and don't call my sponsor. I can easily fake being charismatic and social, but right now, I just don't give a shit. The production is wrapped—I don't want to act anymore. Of course, I'm perfectly aware that the only person suffering here is me. I despise the fact that I often have to work so hard just to fit in and be liked. I suddenly feel like I'm in seventh grade again and I'm reminded of the many tedious lunches I spent eating in a bathroom stall so nobody could see that I didn't have a single friend to share the break with. I wish I could pull a Bilbo Baggins and magically escape from this party without anyone interfering by begging me to stay when they don't really care. Unfortunately, I've left my purse inside, poorly hidden behind the bar, and I can't go anywhere without it.

I slide against the brick wall and inch my way back toward the front door. I narrowly avoid getting back-handed by a skinny, twenty-something boy who flails his arms wildly in an attempt to prove some point that he's failing to make. I lean into the door to push it open but lose my balance when a middle-aged woman in a teenager's dress pulls on it from the inside at the exact same time. Her champagne sloshes onto the concrete below and I find myself caught between her and another woman as they decide to start a conversation in the entry way. I become sandwiched between them, unable to escape their teetering stances and flapping arms. They continue gossiping as I impatiently wait for them to go outside or stay inside or agree to depart in opposite directions. But they don't. I realize that I must be invisible. Perhaps I'm a ghost and I can walk straight through them. That's the only logical explanation. I decide to try, but without success, bumping shoulders with the second woman. She finally acknowledges my existence with a snotty, "Excuse you." I continue past her and once I'm at least five steps away she adds a "bitch."

I'm in a huge loft—a wide open space with ceilings at least thirty feet high. Expensive furniture has been placed intelligently, creating various lounging areas. The golden hardwood floors are only mildly scratched. Each of the three visible walls are painted a different color. One is a deep purple, lined with silver shelves abstractly arranged and containing every device imaginable necessary for a home theater. A flat screen television is centered on the wall and is nearly the size of my four-door sedan. A generic slideshow of photos taken on set during the production plays in crisp high definition. A black leather couch, long enough to fit ten people, provides seating for comfortable viewing. The opposite wall is a pale orange, perhaps a melon. It is lined with rustic brown bookshelves holding enough material to start a library. The far wall is a baby blue, but has been mostly barricaded by two large Japanese silk screens. The area appears to be an office of sorts and leads into a separate room, most likely the kitchen. Almost every inch of leftover wall space contains a framed painting. I don't know fine art, so I can't tell if they're oil or acrylic or charcoal. But they all contain people—the back of a girl standing in a corner, her face against the wall; a young man enviously eyeing an embracing couple; a woman gazing desperately out a window while a man undresses her from behind. The style is messy, smudged and smeared, and avoiding inclusion of small characteristics that would exist in a photo or portrait. They all seem very sad, containing long stories and dark secrets. Absorbing these paintings has been the best part of the night by far.

Even with the forty or so people mingling about, the space doesn't feel too crowded. Not a single person is sitting. They're all standing in small circles, shifting uncomfortably in their high heels and stiff dress shoes. I've never understood why people seem to feel obligated to remain standing at social gatherings. I'm usually the first person to sit my ass down and plant it there for the night. I eye the bar, which appears to be a permanent feature in the corner adjoining the baby blue and the pale orange. A bartender stands behind it—a man in his late-twenties covered in tattoos, his dirty blonde hair gelled into a spiky mess, whom I assume is not permanent. Perhaps he'd be attractive if he weren't bartending for a private cast party. I approach him and his station, careful not to make eye-contact with anyone along the way.

"What can I get for you," he inquires as soon as I'm within his eight-foot radius.

"My purse," I reply dryly.

"I'm sorry?"

"My purse. I was told I could leave it behind the bar."

"Oh, go ahead." He gestures for me to enter his security bubble and cross behind the bar. A small stack of bags and jackets has grown on the floor and I dig through them to find my own. I consider the opportunity literally lying below me—unattended purses and wallets, the bartender having long since forgotten I'm even there. But the thought quickly passes due to my recently developed attention to morals. I locate my purse, a $9.99 black faux leather item from Target at least six seasons old and torn at the edges. I swing it over my shoulder and hastily back out of the bar, anxious to slip out of here, to be free at last!

"Leaving already?"

I recognize that voice. I turn around and find myself face to face with the loud girl from outside. She's gorgeous. She looks like Scarlett Johansson but with roasted almond brown hair cut just below her chin and topped with perfectly even bangs. Her pale ivory skin is flawlessly clear with just a hint of shine in it. Her emerald-green eyes are large and round, straight out of a Japanese anime, and laced with thick black lashes. She has plump, cherry-pink lips that glisten under the light from recently applied gloss and the moisture of her own saliva. She's petite, maybe only a couple inches taller than me, but with more pronounced curves. Her smoky grey tank-top is fitted tightly and barely exposes her collar bone but hangs completely open in the back, attached only by a thin ribbon tied just above her ass. It's obvious she isn't wearing a bra. Her breasts are full and perky, but not too large, so they're proportionate to the rest of her body. Her nipples are hard and erect, protruding through the thinness of her shirt. Her skinny, hip-hugger denims sit low, accentuating her perfectly round butt. She carries herself confidently, comfortable with her own body and proud to show it.

"I've been here for longer than I can handle," I mutter.

"Really?" she sounds genuinely astonished and glances at her watch. "But you've only been here for, maybe, forty-five, fifty minutes."

"Are you stalking me?" I say it more like a tease than a threat.

"I wouldn't call it that. But I saw you come in and thought you looked interesting. So I've been keeping my eye on you here and there."

I think that was a pick-up line. But I'm not quite sure because I'm not used to such articulate attempts.

"I'm extremely anti-social," is my equally uncommon response. "And I don't do well at cast parties."

There's a brief pause as we stare off. She locks eyes with me and I'm immediately entranced by her seductive gaze. I feel flushed and uncomfortable, but I'm too stubborn to look away.

"I'll make you a deal," she finally offers. "You stay and I'll take you upstairs to my studio so you don't have to be around any of these assholes except me."

The next thing I know I'm in a brightly lit room surrounded by every color that the human eye can possibly process. I can hear a low murmur and an occasional bass from the party below me, but I feel as if I've been transported to an entirely new world. The studio is filled with paintings obviously created by the same artist that I was admiring downstairs. The walls are covered with completed works on canvas, some framed and some not. A large artist's desk is stacked with incomplete pieces and sketches drawn on loose paper. Six different easels are standing throughout the room. All but one contains canvasses of various sizes with paintings all showing different levels of progress. Plastic bins and filing cabinets are filled with paints, brushes, pens, pencils, sponges and the like. More tools, blank canvasses, art books and sketch pads are strewn across the floor. I stand in the center of the room, attempting to take it all in but finding myself completely overwhelmed by the beauty surrounding me.

"These are yours?" I eventually exhale. "This is your work?"

I can sense that the girl is behind me, still standing by the door, but I don't turn to face her.

"Yeah," she speaks softly now. "This is my art."

"I love it. This is amazing. This is, I don't know, I don't have words for it."

"Good."

"Where does it come from?" I ask. "I mean, what inspires you to create art like this?"

"I like to expose human emotions through abstract portraits. All of my paintings are of real people, people I know or people I've seen passing by in everyday life. Their initial images are very realistic to what they actually look like. But then I try to bring what I think is occurring on their insides to the outside, capturing stills exposing these individuals in ways they would probably never expose themselves."

Finally, I turn to face her. She's watching me watching her, taking in the entirety of her world. I want to express how awed I am, how inspired I feel, but I can't find the words.

"I like that," is all I come up with. "I like that a lot."

"Thank you."

She approaches me then drops to sit on a large orange and blue shag carpet that I hadn't realized I was standing on. I follow her lead and join her on the floor.

"So, do you live here too?" I inquire.

"Yeah. I live here with my husband."

"Jason's your husband?" I refer to one of the executive producers of the film. He had come on set a couple of times and I knew that we were all at his loft for the cast party.

"Yep. I'm Charlotte." Despite the late, awkward timing, she offers her hand to me, which I shyly shake. "And, of course, I already know who you are. I've seen some of the footage and Jason has raved about you more than once."

"Really?"

"Really. But don't tell him."

"Don't tell him what?"

She leans into me, never losing eye-contact, until our noses are almost touching.

"About this," she whispers. And before the second word has completely left her mouth, she presses her moist lips hard against mine.

She tastes like White Zinfandel and black cherry lip gloss. Her mouth is soft and a pleasant change from the various men I've most recently been seduced by. The kiss is aggressive, but her lips are so tender that the action feels gentle and sensual. This close I can smell a hint of green apple conditioner in her hair. A fluttering sensation grows in my stomach—something I haven't felt since grade school when the boy I had a crush on would glance over at me from the opposite side of the classroom. For some strange reason I feel like I'm experiencing my first kiss ever.

Eventually, she slowly pulls back and looks down at her hands. She picks at the chipped black polish on her nails and giggles awkwardly.

"I'm sorry," she mumbles.

"What for?" I keep my voice at a whisper.

"That was inappropriate. I shouldn't have done that."

"I guess it was a little inappropriate," I tease her. "But it's fine, I liked it."

She keeps her eyes down, embarrassed in an undeniably adorable way. So I make the next move, constructed from visuals of tender moments I've only ever seen in the movies. I gently use the tips of my fingers to lift her chin so we are eye-to-eye again. Then I drag the nail of my index finger across her bottom lip before clasping my hand around the back of her head. I pull her into me and wrap my mouth around hers. I suck on her from various angles. When I feel her teeth part, I slip my tongue into her. She responds and we move together. She feels like warm chocolate melting in my mouth. I clench my fist around a handful of her silky hair and tug on it from the roots. She moans and allows her head to tilt back with my hand, her chin pointing toward the ceiling. I slide my mouth down to her neck and suck on the smooth skin just above her collar bone. I briefly rest my other hand on her shoulder before slipping it down to one of her breasts. Even through her shirt I can feel the distinct point of her erect nipple. I massage her, exploring every inch of her soft tit. It feels absolutely perfect in my hand—the perfect size, the perfect shape, the perfect texture. I feel both her hands on the back of my neck. Her fingernails begin to dig into me as my touch becomes more aggressive. I run my fingers down her stomach until I locate the hem of her shirt. Then I slip my hand under it and return to her chest. Her perfection becomes blatant when I feel the smoothness of her skin. I circle my finger on the tip of her nipple then pinch it hard. She struggles to move her arms past mine so she can lift her shirt off over her head. I sit back for a moment to take her in. Her milky white skin glows under the lights. Her arms and stomach are toned, but just slightly so as not to appear masculine. She has the body that I've always dreamed of owning. But rather than feeling jealous, I feel flattered that she is sharing it with me.

Once my eyes are content, I nuzzle my face back into her neck and suck on her skin. I create a moist trail of licks and kisses along her collar bone and down the center of her chest. I can feel the in and out movement of her lungs increase as her breathing becomes heavier. I continue my journey around the circumference of her left breast. Once I've returned to my starting point, I continue the same pattern around her right, drawing a figure eight across her bust. I can taste a hint of saltiness from microscopic beads of sweat that have begun leaking from her pores. She places both of her hands on my head and massages my scalp with her nails. She runs her fingers through my hair and for a moment I think I'm in grade-school again, playing with a curious girlfriend during a private slumber party. Her touch causes a cold shiver down my spine and my limbs suddenly feel weak. She's discovered my soft spot and she knows how to work it.

As my mind drifts into a state of euphoria, my mouth continues its path. I slide the tip of my tongue toward the center of her right breast and gently lick her nipple, up and down then left and right. Then I inhale it between my lips and suck on its entirety. Her nipple is so erect that I feel like I'm sucking on a small piece of hard candy. Then I take it between my teeth and gently nibble on it before quickly fluttering my tongue against it and returning to long, aggressive sucks. When I move to her left tit to repeat the process, her hands cease their gentle massage on my head. Instead, she grabs a fistful of my hair and yanks my head back and up toward her face again. She presses her mouth hard against mine and swallows me whole. Her kisses are no longer kisses, but rather desperate, lustful attacks, as if she were a hungry lioness feeding on the carcass of a gazelle she worked so hard to kill. I lose control and let her take the lead, only opening my lips wider when I feel appropriate and slipping my tongue into her mouth when I think I can do it fast enough to keep up with her. I can no longer contain my building saliva or my sudden gasps for air. My lips start to feel chaffed and raw. My muscles tense as I yearn for her to move to other parts of my body, but I don't want to offend her by pulling away. Instead, I slip my hand under her shirt and find the waistline of her jeans. I fumble to unbutton and unzip them until I feel the thin, silky material of her panties. I run my finger across the hem before sliding my hand beneath them. Her pubic hair feels soft yet bristly against my skin and I pet it as if it's the top of a kitten's head. Then I slowly yet deliberately work my way down until I reach the base of her clitoris.

"Wait," she exhales, finally releasing her grasp on my mouth. "I'm on my period." She pulls my hand out of her pants and simply holds it for a moment.

"Anyway," she continues, "I just want to make you feel good tonight."

I'm not exactly sure what she means by that, but I figure I'd be stupid to argue. So I sit still and patiently wait for her to guide me. She releases my hand and tugs at the bottom of my shirt. As she lifts it, I assist by raising my arms up until it's over my head and thrown aside on the floor. Then she wraps her arms around me in order to unclasp my bra, which is also thrown out of view. She gently pushes against my bare chest and guides my descent onto the ground until I'm laying flat on my back. I stare at the ceiling, observing the steady rotations of a plain white fan dangling from above. For the first time, I hear the blades of the fan slicing through the air circulating within the room. My eyelids become heavy as I drift into a sort of hypnotic trance. Soon, my eyes grow uncomfortable from the brightness of the lights and I slowly close them.

I drift into an unfamiliar state of innocence and exploration. I have been with women before, but always in a drunken stupor or in a desperate search for affection or in an exhibition solely to entertain a group of men. Usually, all three. But with Charlotte, I feel like I'm indulging in a fantasy with a long-time love I had lost because she became unavailable after someone else won her over first. I allow the weight of my body to sink into the carpet below me and I feel as if I've fallen through the floor boards into an ethereal realm of nothing and everything all at once.

Her fingers swiftly unzip my jeans and she tugs at them. I've become paralyzed, so she places her hands under my ass and lifts me up slightly in order to slip them off my hips. I feel the cool breeze of the ceiling fan tickle my recently shaved pelvis and I realize she's removed my underwear as well. And suddenly I'm left naked on the floor—vulnerable and exposed. I lose sense of her presence for a moment and worry that she's disappeared. But I refuse to open my eyes out of fear that I'll be yanked back into reality, only to find myself still downstairs, behind the bar, digging for my purse. But then I feel a soft peck on my chin. Then another on my neck, then my chest, then my breast. She kisses one of my nipples before sucking on it—soft at first, then harder, then soft again. She gives it a sharp bite and my chest involuntarily convulses. Then she draws circles around it with the tip of her tongue. I open my legs slightly, attempting to remain discreet, to allow the cool breeze to wrap around the moisture seeping from my vagina. But when her lips glide over to my other nipple, I feel a thick drop of wetness slide between my ass.

When her mouth eventually leaves my breasts, I feel abandoned. But only for a moment. Her lips reconnect with my skin, creating a straight line of gentle pecks from the center of my chest down to my belly button. She pauses briefly to slip her tongue inside, then continues her journey down to my pelvis. The moment her lips touch my clit, my body convulses. She ignores my reaction and begins to tease it with her tongue. She starts with long, warm licks, then gradually increases her pace until they become fast, constant flutters. I bend my knees and arch my back to fully expose the most sensitive part of my body to her. She adjusts with me, never ceasing her work. My vagina is throbbing so hard that I'm positive she must be able to feel it. A charge of electricity shoots from between my legs and down to my toes, then bounces back up through my torso and out my finger tips. I feel my orgasm ready to explode right then and there, but I struggle to hold it back because I'm embarrassed by the prospect of coming too fast. Then suddenly, I feel her touch on my erect nipples again. She has reached both her hands up to my breasts and teases then with her soft fingers. The indescribable sensation of being pleasured at both ends of my body throws me into a deepened state of lightheadedness. And without warning, I release a guttural scream as my body suddenly orgasms without my permission. My legs convulse, trying to kick her away from me, unable to handle the erotic explosion. But she stays with me, wanting to follow me all the way through. My back arches desperately, causing a sharp cramp between my shoulder blades. My arms go numb, as if they've been dunked into buckets of ice water. A ball of energy rises to my head, causing my lips and scalp to tingle. I release a final cry as my orgasm peaks but am startled by a sudden knock on the door. Charlotte quickly pulls away from me and my eyes flutter open. The room seems so bright that I become dizzy from it. I can no longer tell if the ceiling fan is still rotating above me, or if it's my body that is spinning on the floor below.

"Okay, I'll be right down." I struggle to lift my head slightly to see Charlotte peeking through a small crack in the door, speaking to an unseen individual. Then suddenly, she's above me again, her lips against mine.

"I have to go say 'good-bye' to Jason's father," she whispers. "I'm sorry we can't lie together a bit longer, but you'll meet me down there, won't you?"

I am unable to open my mouth to speak, but I must have managed a slight nod. And like that, she's gone, and I'm alone, lying naked on the floor. Afraid to accidentally fall asleep, I force myself to rise, stretching and slowly redressing myself. I find myself downstairs again, but I can't remember the climb down. The party has died. Only six or seven people remain mingling inside and I wonder how long we were away. I scour the room, looking for Charlotte. When I don't see her, I look for Jason, but can't find him either. I step outside, assuming that would be the logical place to look. But when I'm hit by the cold night air, I find that the sidewalk outside of the loft is completely empty. There isn't a single human being seen on the block. I eye my car parked on the opposite side of the street, coated in dew. Then suddenly I'm inside of it. I start the engine and blast the heater before lighting up a cigarette and driving home.

The Foreigner

I impatiently tapped my knuckles against the elevator
wall as the doors opened to let the last stranger off. As soon
as my decent to the first floor was complete, I raced past the
convenience store and emerged into the bustling city.
Midnight was quickly approaching, but the bright lights of
Tokyo and the wet August air kept the streets crowded with
pedestrians in the midst of their weeknight excursions. Josh
was there waiting for me, just as anxious, finishing a
cigarette. I could tell that he had grown sweaty rushing from
the train station to the hotel, but he looked as beautiful as
ever. I felt like we were in a movie—one of those shots they
use for love-at-first-sight moments where the crowd and the
lights around us become a blur, moving in super fast or slow
motion, and only the two of us remain in real-time. I pulled
him close to me and pressed my lips hard against his. He
tasted salty, combined with the slightest remnants of a malt
beer and Japanese cigarettes. I let my purse slip off my
shoulder and onto the concrete lining of a decorative hedge.
I wrapped both arms around his neck and pushed my tongue
toward the back of his mouth. His warm wetness caused me
to salivate and a slight tremble shot from under my ribs to
between my legs. I had to tighten the muscles in my crotch
to stop my clitoris from throbbing. As our tongues made love
in our mouths, I slid my left hand down to the bulge in his
pants which had undeniably grown on its own. I tightened

my grasp around the thickness of his jeans and his cock grew harder, bending against the obstacle of clothing. With dozens of people walking by and the bright lights of the surrounding high-rises, I became even more aroused by the fact that Josh didn't brush my hand away. As much as he loves it when I immediately reach for his goods, he's never been a big fan of public displays of affection.

Although we were both in Tokyo, we were each there for different reasons and had been struggling to arrange some private time. That night was our only opportunity to spend completely alone together and we had each done some last minute research in an attempt to take full advantage of our rendezvous on the opposite end of the world. I felt like I was starting a new life in this surreal, fantasy city. Millions of people who all looked alike to me were crammed into such a small geographic region. No matter where I walked, I was surrounded by active beings who all seemed to have purpose. I couldn't understand the language, so my ears weren't bombarded with the negative side comments or ditsy one-dimensional conversations of passing strangers. I was a henna gaijin, a "strange foreigner," because even though I was from overseas, I could blend right in because I looked like them. And in that moment, I felt so alive. I dreaded the fact that I would soon have to return to Los Angeles where reality and normality anxiously awaited.

"Let's go. We don't have much time," I exhaled, planting a final kiss on Josh's wet mouth, but gently keeping my hand cupped over his hardness.

"Okay," he replied. His warm breath tickled my forehead. I grabbed his hand and began to lead the way, but he held me back.

"Wait. I need a minute." He used me as a shield from the public eye as he readjusted himself. He took a couple of deep breaths and shook one leg, which forced me to giggle. I had never met a man before who could be so sexy and so boyishly adorable at the same time. After what seemed like much longer than it was, he swung his backpack over his shoulder and wrapped his arm around me.

"I'm ready," he whispered.

We walked away from the curved, futuristic architecture of the hotel and began our brief journey to the other side of Shinjuku, the most dynamic district in Tokyo. We moved fast, dodging the barriers of other pedestrians, passing dozens of colorful vending machines and air conditioned mini-marts. I observed the young Japanese girls we passed and admired their quirky fashion sense—their high heels, lacy stockings, and long t-shirts which were worn as short dresses and were littered with bad English. We entered the train station, which is a complete community in itself. Salary men rushed past us to catch the last train home after an evening of drinking with their colleagues. Glassy-eyed tourists stood clumped in groups, alternating their focus between the color-coded subway maps and their Lonely Planet guidebooks. I held onto Josh's hand as we dodged the moving obstacles, passing coffee shops and clothing stores, climbing upstairs then riding down escalators. We emerged from the opposite side of the station and into Kabukicho, where we were immediately met by an endless flood of neon lights.

Kabukicho is one of several red light districts in Tokyo. But the area isn't necessarily looked down upon the way it might be in the states. It is simply blocks of high rises filled from top to bottom with restaurants, bars, clubs, arcades and the like. Most of the young Japanese are there for a lively night out on the town. But for those who know exactly which buildings to enter, sex and companionship can undoubtedly be paid for.

I led the way to a location that I had briefly explored earlier. A shadowed flight of stairs began within a concrete door frame on the street and descended to the basement level of a thin building at least ten stories high. Above, aside and in front of the entrance way were a variety of signs and banners advertising "Massage" and prices ranging from 8,000 yen per half hour to 25,000 yen per hour. Color photos of about a dozen young women were stapled onto a wooden stand-alone board that had been pushed half-way into the street. Each photo was labeled with a generic fake name like "Jade" or "Mariko."

"Do you like anything here?" I asked Josh.

"I'll like whatever you like, babe."

I pointed to one of the plainer girls who had kept her hair naturally black and hid her youth only by smearing charcoal liner across her eyelids to her temples. She was labeled as "Lily," which I found ironically amusing since the Japanese language does not include an "L" sound. The parlor was obviously aimed toward foreign visitors—more specifically, Americans.

"You like her?" Josh smirked.

"Mmhmm."

"She kind of looks like you."

"No she doesn't," I argued. "That would be creepy."

"She does," he shot back. "Except the black hair and she doesn't have freckles. But with all the black eye make-up, there's definitely a resemblance."

"Well, let's just go inside. Or else we'll end up standing out here all night." I grabbed his hand and began to pull him toward the staircase, but again, he held me back.

"Come here," he mumbled. He pulled me into his warm body and pressed his lips firmly against mine. "I love you."

"I love you, too," I whispered. A huge grin developed on his face as if he were a small boy who had been told that just this once he could have a cookie before dinner.

Halfway down the stairs a bell sounded and an older Japanese woman poked her head out from a door at the bottom. She looked up to greet us with a yellow smile.

"Konbanwa!" her voice was shrill. "Come in." She placed two pairs of slippers on the floor and gestured toward a small shoe shelf pushed up against the wall. Josh and I complied, awkwardly removing our shoes before entering the parlor. Large curtains had been strewn together to block off the majority of the room. Sheets, towels, lotions and oils were stacked on various tables and in plastic bins scattered about. A large, bald man sat on a stool far too small for him near the entrance. He acknowledged us with a simple nod and grunt. Another silhouette enveloped in a thick cloud of cigarette smoke was barely visible in a small hallway leading to another room.

"You American?" the woman directed her question at Josh.

"Hai," he replied.

"Good. We like Americans."

Between Josh's minimal Japanese and the woman's severely broken English, the two of them struggled to discuss whether or not Josh and I would be able to receive our massages side-by-side at the same time. Once it was apparently confirmed, the woman retrieved a small stack of laminated papers and offered them to us. Each sheet contained various photos of a girl and her alias. I recognized some of the faces from the poster outside, but we were also provided with full-body shots of the girls in skimpy outfits and in seductive poses. We were only given four girls to choose from, so I was happy to find Lily included in the stack.

"Mine," I yanked her photo out of Josh's hand.

"I know, I know," he teased. "You have to help me choose one."

Normally I didn't prefer Asian girls, partly because I'm Asian and it would only increase my need to be competitive. And partly because I'm Asian and for most of my life I had wished I wasn't. But in Tokyo, I didn't have a choice.

We held our remaining three options in front of us. Two were bleach blonde and the other kept her black hair in a cute chin-length bob. I grabbed one of the blondes who had also smeared her face in teal eye shadow, orange blush and pink lipstick, and put her aside.

"Too much make-up," I commented.

"Yeah," Josh agreed. "I was about to say she was my least favorite."

We eyed the other two girls. Both were petite, which I liked, but the black-haired girl had huge breasts that were disproportioned to the rest of her body. I normally didn't prefer large breasts either. Partly because I'm flat-chested and have always wished I wasn't. And partly because I always believed that big boobs only look good when they're still in a bra, and their nipples tend to be stretched out and unattractive.

I pulled the black-haired girl out of Josh's hand and threw her aside as well.

"Okay, her," I referred to the blonde. Her photo was labeled as "Keiko."

"Awesome," Josh replied. "The other one's boobs are too big."

I smiled but didn't admit out loud that he had read my mind. God, I love my boyfriend.

We offered our selections to the woman, who eagerly took the menus back from us and pushed us toward the curtained area.

"Hai, hai. Good, good," she smiled. She handed the photos to the silhouette in the hallway and followed us to the other side of the curtains.

Josh and I found ourselves in a small square. Three sides were enclosed by the drapes and the wall before us contained a large mirror. Two massage tables sat side-by-side, lined with fresh white sheets. A robe was neatly folded on each bed. The woman retrieved two plastic bins and gestured for us to place our bags in them.

"Pajamas," she pointed to the robes. "Okay," she smiled and quickly left.

Josh and I locked eyes, huge grins on both our faces, filled with excitement and nervousness. He reached for me, pulled me into his body, and placed a soft, warm kiss on my lips.

"I love you," he whispered.

"I love you, too."

We watched each other undress and slip into the robes.

"Are you going to keep your underwear on?" he asked.

"Um, yeah, for now. Just in case." In case of what, I didn't know.

"Okay, me too."

"I'm not going to tie my robe, though," I added. "Since we'll be lying on our stomachs first anyway."

"Yeah, that's true. I'm just going to do whatever you do. You lead the way."

We sat on our tables, facing each other. We played footsy, awkwardly waiting to be told what to do next.

"The mirror is kind of weird," Josh commented.

"Why?"

"Do you think it's a two-way mirror?"

"Probably."

"What?"

"I mean, yeah. You know, they might want a way to keep an eye on things."

My theory made perfect sense to me, but Josh shifted uncomfortably. "Sumimasen!" he called out.

I heard footsteps respond immediately and the woman poked her head through the curtains. "Hai?"

"Uh, kamera wa achira desu ka?" Josh pointed to the mirror. "Is there a camera?"

"Camera?" the woman asked.

"Hai."

"Oh, no, no," she laughed. "No camera."

"Okay," Josh released an awkward chuckle. "Sumimasen. Arigato."

The woman bowed her head and left. I swung my legs back and forth off the side of the massage table, as my feet couldn't quite reach the floor. Josh and I kept our eyes locked on one another until we were interrupted by the swift sounds of the curtains opening. Lily entered, followed by Keiko, who closed the drapes behind her. Both were dressed almost identically—lingerie and a short, sexy kimono-style robe. Lily wore a matching bra and panties, a simple, translucent design of black lace with just a hint of red peeking out from the areas that were meant to remain covered. Her short robe was also a mesh of red and black, interweaved to create a pattern of bamboo and lilies.

Red and black are my colors too! I thought to myself. Maybe Josh is right—she's just like me. Josh was most likely thinking the exact same thing, although I never would have mentioned it. To myself, I realized that I must be quite conceited to have chosen a girl who was so similar to me on the outside. I should have given her to Josh. Then it would have been like two of me touching him instead of another woman.

Keiko was in a thin piece of light pink lingerie with spaghetti straps that sat loosely on her shoulders and a lacy hem that didn't quite cover her ass. She had curled her long, blonde hair and pulled it back into a clip which allowed the ends to bounce just above her breasts. Her robe was a baby blue with a large yellow crane perched in sea green plants stitched across the back and down to the hem on both sides. I felt confident that Josh and I had selected the right girls.

They did not speak to us, but simply gestured their instructions. Lily came to the side of my bed and motioned her arm in a way that I interpreted as "Lay down." I obliged, stretching out flat on my stomach and adjusting my face to fit comfortably into the head rest. I saw that Josh was doing the same just before I closed my eyes and allowed myself to slip into a state of nothingness.

I heard shuffling from all sides of the room, both inside and outside of the curtains. The steady hum of the air conditioner only slightly masked occasional murmurs between the woman, the big man and the silhouette. The smell of a freshly lit cigarette engulfed the tiny space and tickled my nostrils. Lily gently grabbed the collar of my robe and tugged at it. I shifted my body to help her slip it off my shoulders, then my arms, then my back, and fold it across my hips. I heard the shuffling of feet, the opening of drawers, the placement of bottles, then the lathering of body oil as two small hands rubbed together. I waited impatiently for Lily to place her palms on me, wondering where they would land first.

She started in the center of my back, between my shoulder blades. Every pore of my skin felt the warm tingle of the oil as she pushed her weight up toward my neck. Huge knots had developed throughout my upper back from nearly two weeks of trucking around luggage. I couldn't help but moan softly as her hands stumbled over those spots, dug into them briefly, then moved on. She worked her knuckles and elbows into me, then drove the sore energy outwards and down my sides with her palms again. I couldn't see him, but I could hear periodic moans escape from Josh's lips and knew that he was experiencing the same satisfaction I was. After a brief pause to re-lather, I sensed some extra weight on the massage table as Lily joined me on top of it. She grabbed my waist to balance herself as she climbed on me and straddled my ass. The warmness of her bare inner thighs teased me around the edges of my underwear. As she rocked back and forth to apply various levels of pressure into my back, I felt the lips of my vagina begin to throb and a small puddle of wetness form. She continued working my back and neck, then my arms one by one before she rose slightly to turn around and work my legs and feet. As I felt myself drifting into a state of sleep and complete euphoria, she dismounted me and, once again, stood off to the side.

Although her skin was no longer touching mine, the throbbing in my pussy only increased. She slowly lifted my robe and hinted for me to put it back on. I obeyed, though somewhat begrudgingly, and looked up until I could really see her face for the first time. She was pretty within her minimal make-up and long, black hair. Her skin was perfectly smooth without a hint of a blemish. Her lips were full and glossy and her eyes contained a definite trace of youth and innocence behind them. She couldn't have been more than twenty, maybe twenty-one. She caught me staring at her and released a soft giggle.

"Okay?" she asked timidly.

"Huh?" was my suave reply.

"It's okay?"

"Yes. Hai."

She made another motion with her arm to instruct me to turn over. I struggled to get my limp, lazy muscles to do so. When I finally made it onto my back, one side of my robe slipped open, completely exposing my right breast. I left it there. Lily stood directly behind me and worked her fingertips into my scalp, then my temples and my ears. I peered out of the corners of my eyes and saw that Josh was just turning over and resettling onto his back. He had chosen not to put his robe back on and laid there on top of it in nothing but his boxer-briefs. Once Lily had worked her way down to my chest, I turned my head to face Josh. We caught eyes and simultaneously smiled. He turned back so that Keiko could massage his head, but I kept watching. He looked so content, so at peace, so beautiful.

I was pulled out of my trance when I felt Lily's palm brush against my already hard nipple. She opened my robe so I was fully exposed and rubbed her hands around the circumference of my breasts. Occasionally, her thumb or index finger would bump into my erect nipples, which I was sure she was doing on purpose. I was proven correct when she ceased the massage and simply used her two index fingers to tease them. I inhaled deeply and focused all of my attention on the softness of her touch. Suddenly, she pulled both hands away and I almost protested. But her fingertips soon returned, wet with her saliva. I moaned and flexed the muscles between my legs in an unsuccessful attempt to ease the throbbing of my vagina.

I felt Josh's gaze on me again so I turned to him. The look on his face told me that he was ready for more and I nodded in agreement. I wasn't sure if we needed to ask or if the girls would just lead the way. And even if I could speak their language, I still didn't think I'd know what to say. But I didn't want our hour to run out while I contemplated this obstacle. So I communicated in the same way they did—through movement. I lifted my ass so I could slip my panties off and kicked them to the floor. Then I bent my knees and straddled my legs, opening myself up to whatever wanted to enter. I heard both girls giggle and I was suddenly embarrassed by the stubble that had grown around my pussy. But then I realized it probably didn't matter in Japan. I watched Josh as he followed my lead and also slipped himself out from his underwear. His cock had already grown and was gradually lifting its head to the ceiling.

I could see the girls moving around but couldn't tell exactly what they were doing. For a moment I was afraid that we had made the wrong move, that this was all a misunderstanding. But then Lily reappeared at the foot of my bed with something in her hand. It was a small vibrator—the kind you could slip on your finger, no larger than a lighter, with a ribbed tip. She locked eyes with me.

"Okay?" she smiled seductively.

"Hai," I choked out.

I looked back at Josh as I heard the soft hum of the vibrator start up. His eyes were focused between my legs as Lily placed the toy on the tip of my clit and slowly began to move it back and forth. My entire body tensed up, my muscles finally coming back to life. She knew exactly where to work it—on the most sensitive part of my clit without adding too much additional pressure. I arched my back to pull away slightly so I wouldn't come too fast. She used her other hand to continue the massage, pinching and rubbing my inner thighs. I reached out to Josh and he clasped onto my hand without hesitation. I tried to pull him closer without any success. Keiko witnessed my attempt and she ducked under Josh's massage table. I heard two soft clicks then she reappeared and pushed on the table until it rolled up against mine, making our two beds into one. Two more clicks. I shifted my upper body so I could rest my head on Josh's shoulder. I held onto his hand, tightening my grip as the tickle of the vibrator grew more intense. I heard the lathering of oil between two palms again. I lifted my chin so I could kiss Josh. We opened our mouths, sucking in each other's breath. Our tongues caressed and danced and tumbled until they were interrupted by a low groan from the back of his throat. His mouth froze but didn't leave mine. I pulled away and looked down to see that Keiko had wrapped her fist around his cock. She moved her hand slowly, back and forth from the base to the tip, oil seeping from between her fingers. I watched it jump in her hands, bouncing slightly like a pin in a carnival game that has been weighted at the bottom so it's impossible to knock over. Josh's hardness had grown to its full extent and my wetness had soaked the sheets beneath me. He turned onto his shoulder, released my hand, and grabbed onto both sides of my face. He pulled me in anxiously and shoved his tongue back into my mouth. We kissed hard, passionately, biting, sucking. We tickled each other's mouths with our moans and groans and grunts. Lily never ceased with the toy, so I kept readjusting myself, changing the location of the vibrations so I could hold back and come at the same time as Josh. Then she slipped her finger inside of me and moved it in circles. I could feel her long fingernail brushing against the walls of my tunnel. When she added a second finger, she banged me more aggressively and increased the pressure of the vibrator against my clit. I bit Josh's lower lip to prevent myself from screaming out. He maintained his grip on me and pressed his forehead against mine.

"I love you," he panted, his mouth dry and his voice raspy.

"I love you," I exhaled back.

Then he pushed me so I was flat on my back again. He rotated his upper body to lean into me and wrapped his lips around my nipple. He sucked on it, nibbled on it, then used his warm, wet tongue to draw circles around it. I lifted my head slightly and saw that Keiko was diligently jerking him off. Her pace had increased and she was using the fingertips of her other hand to massage his balls. I felt Lily remove her fingers and walk from the end of the bed to my side. She kept the toy on me but leaned her face in and vacuumed my other nipple into her mouth. I watched her and Josh devour me together, the tops of their heads periodically bumping into one another. A burning sensation shot from my clit, down my legs, and into my feet. My pussy pulsated violently, gushing liquids out of its mouth. I arched my back until my weight sat only on my ass and the top of my head. I focused on Josh's thick tongue gyrating against my left nipple and Lily's soft lips sucking on my right. I focused on the sensation of the vibrator moving up and down then left and right. I flexed my thighs, my calves, my feet. I grabbed Josh by the hair and pulled hard on his scalp.

"Oh fuck, oh fuck, oh fuck..." I panted over and over again. My body wanted to orgasm, but my thoughts weren't ready yet. It wasn't the way I had envisioned it.

"Wait!" I gasped.

"What?" Josh pulled away and looked at me, concerned. "What's the matter?"

I gently placed my hand on Lily's, which was in control of the toy, and moved it away. She turned it off and patiently stood to the side.

"Nothing," I replied. "I just don't want to come yet. We're supposed to come together, remember?"

"Of course."

I noticed that Keiko had also paused with her task and stood up. She glanced from me to Josh to Lily, unsure of what had happened.

I sat up and slowly got onto my hands and knees. I crawled the short distance to Josh, my body perpendicular to his, my face level with his crotch. Then I leaned forward and slipped the entirety of his erection into my mouth. The oil soaking his skin tasted of honey, but it was soon replaced with the saltiness of my own saliva. With every upward movement, I pressed my tongue hard against his cock then massaged the area just under the head before descending back down. When I paused to catch my breath I made eye contact with Keiko. I pointed to her, then to my tongue, then to Josh's genitals. She simply nodded her head and re-approached us. She leaned on her elbows at the foot of the bed and obediently stuck her head between Josh's legs. She gingerly slid her tongue across his balls then looked at me for approval. I nodded with a smile then took Josh back into my mouth. I watched Keiko steadily lick him, sometimes sucking one ball into her mouth, then the other, then licking again. I found that I couldn't take his cock in its entirety without getting in her way, so I focused on the tip, sucking on it gently, then hard, then flicking my tongue in the small crevice on the underside. Josh grabbed a fistful of my hair and held on tight, but didn't push. He moaned euphorically while Keiko and I continue our teamwork. Soon, I felt a light touch on the skin between my vagina and my asshole. At first I thought a breeze from the air conditioner had brushed the wetness still dripping between my legs. But when I looked, still on my hands and knees with my ass high in the air, I saw Lily's thighs, bent over waist, and the tops of her breasts protruding from her bra. Then I realized the touch was the tip of her nose bumping against me as she stretched her tongue out to tease my pussy. She repetitively completed full, long licks, poking the underside of my clit with the tip of her tongue, then sliding the bulk of its wetness across my vagina. Sometimes she would drag it all the way up between the crack of my ass then let it rest on my opening.

"Baby," Josh moaned. "I'm getting close."

I gave him one last hard suck then pulled away. I motioned to Keiko to take over and she immediately complied. Then I laid on my back next to Josh, the full length of the sides of our bodies connected. I spread my legs, resting one knee on his thigh. Then I looked to Lily, who had already read my mind. She stood at the end of the massage table, parallel to Keiko, then obediently continued licking me. The tip of her tongue fluttered quickly against the underside of my clit. Then she dragged the thickest part of it across the entire area between my legs. She slipped it inside of me then pulled back out and sucked on me. She continued alternating between her various tactics, playing with different speeds and pressures. I caught glimpses of Keiko swallowing Josh's cock, then taking it in her hand while she sucked on his balls. Josh and I watched our girls work together—my eyes on him, his eyes on me. Simultaneously, we turned to face each other and locked lips once again. The softness of his tongue only accentuated the sensation of the tongue between my legs. We moaned together, inhaling each other's exhales.

"I'm holding back, baby," he murmured without pulling away. "Tell me when." The vibration of his voice tickled my lips.

"Almost, baby. Almost." I arched my back and gyrated my hips in a dance with Lily's mouth. Josh placed one hand on my neck and used the other to tease my nipples. He could rub both at the same time using his thumb and index finger. My legs and back cramped as ecstasy flowed into every corner of my body. Lily shoved her fingers inside of me and banged me hard, her knuckles slamming against my bones, causing my lower body to shake uncontrollably.

"I'm gonna come," I exhaled into Josh's mouth.

"Oh yeah, baby," he moaned. "I want you to come for me."

Our mouths stayed connected and our tongues remained tangled as our panting increased. Our moans vibrated into the backs of each other's throats. We didn't detach, even when we cried out together as we both orgasmed. When I came, I felt a stream of wetness shoot out of my pussy. I had to use my foot to gently push Lily away when she didn't stop licking me. Together, Josh and I convulsed, rapidly at first then less and less as we both recovered. Through blurry vision, I saw Lily bow slightly then leave. Keiko followed, one hand cupped in front of her, which I realized was filled with Josh's cum. She pointed to a stack of neatly folded towels on a nearby night stand, then exited, closing the curtains behind her.

I stared at the ceiling and struggled to catch my breath. I felt Josh's body twitch as he attempted to do the same. We laid there together in silence before he finally crawled on top of me and kissed me. It was a gentle kiss—the kind filled with love rather than lust.

"That was amazing," he whispered. "I love you."

"I love you, too."

He pulled me in close and we slowly drifted into each other's arms.

"I want you to fuck me now," I broke the silence.

"Here?"

"No, silly. I think they want us to leave now. But next I need you to fuck me."

"Okay."

We helped each other up. I had to put my head between my knees before standing to stop the room from spinning. My body was still recovering. We used the towels to wipe ourselves down then stumbled back into our clothes. We collected our belongings and emerged from behind the curtains where the older woman was waiting with an ear-to-ear grin.

"Happy?" she asked.

"Hai," we responded in unison.

I stepped outside to retrieve my shoes and waited for Josh in the entrance way while he took care of the payment. Then we limped up the stairs, hand in hand, and returned to the humid air and bright lights of the outside world.

Josh was in charge of the second half of the night and had done some prior research online. Within the red light districts throughout Tokyo there are businesses known as Love Hotels. They are specifically made available for the purpose of sex, although they are also known to be useful for individuals who simply want to spend a quiet night alone. They can be checked into for a "rest" (several hours) or a "stay" (overnight) and range anywhere from 4,000 yen to 20,000 yen depending on the amount of time requested, the location and the room. In Kabukicho, there is a length of several blocks lined with nothing but Love Hotels. After a couple of wrong turns and uneducated guesses, Josh and I found ourselves standing at the entrance of this district. Rows and rows of neon signs flashed tacky names such as "Hotel Paradise" and "Passion Hotel." Information on rates and times were made available on signs and placards outside of each building. We made our way up the street, looking for options within our price range before venturing inside to view the available rooms. In each hotel lobby, photographs of the vacant rooms were displayed on large electronic screens. No two rooms were exactly alike, varying in shape, size, theme, color, furniture and additional features such as karaoke or a sauna. Josh and I entered and exited nearly a dozen hotels before we finally found a room that appealed to both of us and wouldn't cost a full week's pay. The photograph displayed wooden furniture stained a chocolate brown, including a large bed placed almost center stage with mirrors hanging on the walls around it. The tone of the room was dark and sensual, yet elegant and classy at the same time. I pushed a button labeled "Stay" on the electronic screen. I heard a ding, the photograph disappeared, and a young woman's voice greeted us from a nearby window. She took our payment, told us our check-out time, and then gave us a key. We took the elevator up to the seventh floor and quickly found our room at the end of the hallway. The number was flashing red above the door as if to say, "Come in! Come in!"

"This isn't actually a key," Josh said.

"What do you mean?" I looked in his hand and saw that the large key holder we were given was just that—a holder, with the room number printed on the end of it.

"I guess that means we lock it from the inside and once we're in, we're in," he concluded.

"Fine by me."

The room was huge—more than three times the size of the "real" hotel I was staying in for the remainder of my trip. In addition to the bed and mirrors we were already expecting, there was a large flat screen television, a leather love seat, a coffee table, a vanity area and a small vending machine stocked with water, soda, beer and an assortment of vibrators. The shower contained a deep jet bath tub and a sauna.

"This is fucking awesome!" Josh squealed.

I laughed at his child-like excitement but the ear-to-ear grin on my face proved that I agreed. Then I hastily removed all of my clothing, let my hair down, and fell backwards onto the bed, naked and vulnerable. Josh took his time, stumbling through a dorky striptease, sticking out his perfectly round, soft butt, which he knew I adored. I noticed that he had recently shaved his chest and his genitals, leaving his skin shiny and smooth. Just admiring his perfection made me feel beautiful knowing that I belonged to him and him to me. Then he climbed on top of me and locked his lips around mine. He kissed my neck, my cheeks, my forehead, then returned to my lips. I kept still, allowing each peck he placed on me to sink into the depths of my pores. I could feel the largeness of his cock becoming erect again as it laid between my thighs.

"What should we do first?" he asked.

"Let's take a bath," I suggested in the softer, higher pitched voice I only use when I'm alone with him.

"Okay." He pecked each of my nipples before helping me up and guiding me to the shower. In Japan, the shower is a room in itself and includes a bath tub within it, so we were able to run the water for both at the same time. And the bath is used for relaxing, rather than washing, so it is the norm to shower before stepping into the tub. I began running the bath and added bubbles that I had found in cute packages alongside body wash and lotion. Josh ran the shower and stood still under the warm stream. When I joined him, he pulled me in close and just held me while the water ran over us and between us, then down our bodies and onto the tile below. We rinsed ourselves of Lily and Keiko—their scent, their sweat, their saliva—so it could just be the two of us again. He lathered his hands with soap and massaged his smooth palms all over my body. He started with my neck and worked his way down. He leaned in to take one of my nipples into his mouth, sucking on it then fluttering his tongue against it, before cleansing it. Then he did the same to the other. His touch caused a tingling sensation in my skin as he rubbed his hands into my stomach then turned me around so he could do my back. He moved down to my ass, which he pinched and slapped, then slipped his hand between my legs. He slowly pushed his palm back and forth then used his finger to reach between the lips of my vagina. His touch was so familiar to me, yet it never ceased to send a pleasant shock from between my legs and outward in all directions. He teased my clit, keeping his motions slow and sensual, before finally rubbing down my legs and washing my feet. He helped me rinse, then I started to bathe him. I copied his method, starting at his neck then working my way down. I took in every part of his body that I touched, admiring his strong arms, his smooth back, and the curved shape of his ribs above his stomach. He was truly the epitome of beauty and sexuality. I took his ass in both my hands and just held it for a moment, before sliding my fingertips around his hips and to his genitals. I massaged his balls, allowing the soap and water to work as a warm lubricant. His moans were drowned out by the shower, but the tip of his cock immediately began to lift toward the ceiling. I wrapped my fist around his erection and slid my hand up and down it. I let the water rinse away the soap before dropping to my knees and sliding him into my mouth. His cock had a squeaky-clean texture to it causing my lips to occasionally stick to his skin. I kept my eyes closed as the shower streamed over both of us. I was afraid to inhale through my nose and instead pulled away every five or six strokes, gasping for air through my mouth. Each time I released him the head of his penis would bounce and brush the tip of my nose. I thought about Keiko, wondering if she wished she could taste my boyfriend again. I continued to work my neck back and forth while ungracefully rubbing down his legs and feet.

"All done," I stood up.

"No," he whined.

"The bath is going to overflow!" I exclaimed, which wasn't a lie as the bubbles had begun to spill over the edge of the tub.

Josh sulkily rinsed himself off and joined me at the bath. I timidly placed one foot into the steaming hot water, then the other, then carefully sat down. I felt an instant sweat come over me. Josh followed and we sat facing each other, our legs intertwined. After fiddling with some knobs and switches on the wall, the jets started up, vibrating against my back and between my legs. We sat there in silence, droopy eyed and limp, as if we had just shared a blunt.

"I want to shave you," Josh eventually proclaimed.

"Right now?" I asked.

"Yeah. There's a razor right there."

I turned my head and saw that among the packaged goodies placed neatly near the tub, there was, indeed, a disposable razor.

"Okay." I emerged from the bubbles, sat on the edge of the tub and spread my legs. Josh retrieved the razor and a small package of lotion. I closed my eyes and leaned my head against the wall. I felt him rub the lotion into my pubic hair. I felt the razor glide across my skin. I felt his fingers moving the folds of my vagina from side to side so he could reach every crevice. The pressure of the blade was so subtle that it tickled. Sometimes, between strokes, Josh would slip a finger inside of me and my pussy would expand, reaching for more, until it was repositioned again to be shaved. When he had finished his work, he rinsed me off and slipped his tongue inside of me. He licked me from front to back, nibbled on my clit and drowned me in his saliva. My vagina pulsated, sucking him in but wanting so much more. It wanted to be fucked.

"Let's go to the bed," I interrupted him, closing my legs. "I want you inside of me."

He agreed without speaking and stepped out of the tub. He lifted me onto him, my arms wrapped around his neck and my legs wrapped around his waist. He carried me out of the shower and threw me onto the bed, still soaking wet and covered in bubbles. He kneeled above me and immediately shoved his cock into my pussy. My wetness allowed him to easily slide inside of me in one smooth motion. My vagina clamped around him desperately, only loosening its grip briefly when it throbbed in satisfaction. I grabbed onto the skin of his back as our bones slammed against each other. The sheets beneath me began to tangle and fold as the force of his hips progressively pushed me to the edge of the bed. I let my head fall backward until it was upside down, unsupported. I could see our reflection in one of the mirrors—my head and loose hair, my open thighs and bent knees. His bare torso, flexed arms, and clenched jaw. We looked beautiful together. We looked beautiful when we were one. I imagined that we were shooting a porn flick and that I was watching us in the playback monitor. His cock filled every inch of my crevice. His balls bounced against my ass. His pelvis teased my clit. I didn't want him to stop—ever—but suddenly, he did. He collapsed on top of me.

"Oh my God, you feel so good," he panted. "I almost came. I don't want to come yet."

"I don't want you to come yet either."

"Okay." He slowly caught his breath then sat back up, partially sliding out of me. "I brought something for us to do." He crawled off the bed to retrieve his backpack from the other side of the room.

"Baby..." I whined.

"It'll just take a second." He pulled out a small hand-held video camera and proudly displayed it. "This way I can watch you even after you're gone."

I giggled at the undeniable sensuality of his dorky excitement, trying to hide the fact that I was just as eager to put ourselves on tape. While Josh inspected the camera, making sure it was ready to record, I rose to stretch my legs and explore the vending machine. It contained at least half a dozen vibrators to choose from, ranging in prices that were at least triple what they were worth. They all looked the same to me from the opposite side of the glass, so I selected the cheapest one. I pressed the button below the appropriate compartment and the door to it popped open. I impatiently unwrapped the packaging, installed the batteries, then returned to the bed.

"Ready?" I asked.

"Yep." He joined me.

"I want to go first." I grabbed the camera from him and placed it on the ledge at the head of the bed, between us and a large mirror on the wall. I rotated the viewfinder so I could watch us from two different perspectives at the same time. Then I positioned myself on my hands and knees, my ass facing Josh.

"Let's do it like this," I proposed.

He responded in agreement by sliding himself inside of me again. His erection hadn't decreased in the slightest and was still coated in my wetness. In this position I could feel the head of his cock slamming into new walls within me. Sometimes my stomach flinched from a sudden sharp pain when Josh forced himself deep into unexplored areas. But I held my ground, determined to be the girl that could give him anything he wanted. I wanted to be the girl that fulfilled every one of his sexual desires. I braced myself against the ledge so I wouldn't slip away from him and watched us perform on camera. Most of the frame was a close-up of me. My long, dark hair covered half my face. My eyes, traced in smeared black liner, stared straight back at me. I rocked back and forth, in sync with Josh's vigorous grinding. My small breasts hung downward, nipples hard, bouncing in rhythm. I looked sexy on camera with Josh fucking me, and felt a tinge of guilt for the egocentricity of becoming even more aroused by looking at myself. Between my spread legs, I could see Josh's knees sinking into the sheets. His genitals swung freely, his hands clenched around my ass. I could make out the deep indents that shaped his pelvis and the lines in his stomach created by his flexed muscles. As I watched him fuck me, I truly believed that we must be the sexiest couple on the planet.

We moved into various positions, playing with what looked best on camera and in the mirrors around us. He stretched out on his back and I sat on top of him, bracing my feet on the bed and my elbows on my knees in order to slide up and down his vertical erection. We sat facing each other, rocking in unison, until he grabbed me by the waist and flung me back and forth on his lap, never sliding out of me. We stood on the floor and bent over the bed together, him behind me again, pulling hard on my hair until I was forced to stare at the ceiling. The burning sensation on my scalp caused my pussy to tighten its grip around his cock. We played with speed, pressure and angles. We swallowed each other's spit and sweat. We danced together as if the whole world were watching before finally collapsing back into missionary style.

"I want you to come," Josh whispered in my ear.

This time I responded in agreement by grabbing the vibrator I had purchased and placing the tip of its egg-shaped attachment on my clit. Josh never ceased rocking inside of me, and the added sensation of the toy caused my pussy to throb wildly. Every back and forth repetition of his cock sent a chill down my legs and up to my stomach. My wetness began to soak the sheets below me. Josh increased his pace and his power, slamming hard against my insides, reaching the deepest point he could, then forcing himself in even deeper. When he leaned in to suck on my nipples, I imagined that his lips belonged to Lily and that she was bent over me, my breasts in her mouth and hers in mine. I spit in my hand then stretched my arm under my thighs until I could reach Josh's balls and lathered them with my saliva. I imagined that my hand was Keiko's tongue licking his genitals as they bounced against my ass. I imagined that as we made love, we had our two girls back in bed with us to service us as our own personal sex toys. My feet went numb as my orgasm approached the surface. It felt as if millions of electrical shocks were sparking in every pore, every muscle, every vein of my body. It was so intense I feared I couldn't handle it, that I would suddenly go into shock and my heart would stop beating. It was too much, but I didn't want it to end. When I came, I convulsed, attempting to grab onto Josh's arms or neck or waist, but unable to grip onto anything. I screamed out incoherently, beating my head and hands against the bed. I had lost all control of my body and could do nothing but give into it entirely. I felt the peak of my orgasm, but Josh didn't stop. He fucked me even harder, faster, rougher. And I kept coming, over and over and over again, an orgasm that lasted longer than I ever imagined possible. I threw the vibrator aside, struggling to turn it off. Through teary, blurred vision, I watched Josh's face contort into euphoric desperation that signified he was about to come too. When he did, our bodies flailed against one another as if we were loosely strapped side-by-side on a wild rollercoaster ride filled with endless twists and loops and vertical drops. His sperm filled me and rushed through every path it could take, hitting me like a heroin fix. It overflowed, spilling out of me, and soaked our connected skin, as if to glue us together. Josh collapsed on top of me, our sweaty bodies suctioning onto one another. We both froze, attempting to recuperate. Occasionally, one of us would twitch, causing the other to do the same.

"I love you," I struggled to choke out.

"I love you, too," he whispered back.

"I'm in love with you."

He stayed inside of me as we laid there in silence. I felt his cock make itself comfortable in my warm tightness. It felt like it belonged there permanently, as if it were a part of my own body. I never wanted to let it go. I would never let him go.

We were woken at 8:00 AM the next morning by the piercing buzz of the hotel alarm clock. I was supposed to be back at the "real" hotel for breakfast at 8:30 and surrendered to the fact that I'd be late. Josh and I stumbled into the shower then into our clothes. We took pictures of the room for our scrapbooks and packed all of the unused, disposable items to take as souvenirs. When we rode the elevator back down to the lobby, we were greeted by a hand sticking out of the window of the front desk. We returned the key holder, paid the additional costs accumulated by the vending machine, then stepped back into the real world.

The Tokyo streets were already busy with movement. The sky was overcast, but the humidity caused a warm dampness through the air. We retraced our steps to the other side of Shinjuku station and back to my hotel. We sat outside to share a cigarette before saying the good-byes we were both desperately trying to avoid. But like all good fantasies, this one had to come to an end too.

"I'll see you back in L.A." I muttered, determined not to cry.

"Only two-and-a-half more weeks," he added.

I nodded before pulling him in for a long hug. We kissed, keeping our lips locked while slowly backing away from each other. After several failed attempts, we finally turned around and began to walk in opposite directions. When I reached the sliding glass doors of the hotel I turned back to watch him blend into the mass of pedestrians. He flashed me one last seductive smile before disappearing into the vivid blur of Tokyo.

The Girlfriend

I refuse to let myself fall in love. I'm afraid of how much it will hurt when I hit the ground, and I don't know if I'd be able to pick myself up again. I've fallen in lust and I've fallen in like. Those were always bad enough. I don't ever want to fall in love. But this one—he is so beautiful. No matter how hard I try to pull away, I find myself only getting closer to him. It hurts to be here when I could be over there. But I know that once I'm with him, I won't want to leave. And I'll yearn for the impossible, like the stopping of time. But the truth is inevitable—the sun will always rise, tomorrow will become today, and holding him in my arms will never pay my rent. I honestly don't know if this is good or if this is bad.

Our first date was exceptional. I went into it with the full intention of dissecting all of his flaws. I succeeded because he didn't have many, but I was determined to expand every little nuance into the worst possible defect. I wanted to ensure that, no matter what, it wouldn't work out. His first strike occurred before the date officially began. He was late. Granted, he called me to tell me that he was sitting in traffic and that he'd arrive soon. He apologized profusely over the phone, then again when I met him outside shortly thereafter. His truck was pulled up against a red curb, hazard lights blinking. He was standing on the grass next to the passenger-side door with his hands in his pockets. When I dismounted the final step leading out of my apartment complex he slowly walked towards me. His movements were graceful—confident but not cocky. He wore a humble grin that convincingly stated that he was embarrassed by his tardiness yet happy to see me. When I looked him in the eyes, I suddenly felt shy, as if I were a young school girl who had been caught sneaking a peek at her handsome English teacher during class. Perhaps I was overwhelmed by the unexpected attraction I felt toward him. Or perhaps I didn't want him to see too much of me too soon. So I alternated my focus between his forehead and his nose, and attempted to minimize the spread of my smile so I wouldn't blush. He extended his hand to me, and when I took it, he pulled me in for a hug. Instinctually, I lifted my chin and leaned in as close to his neck as possible without causing an awkward invasion of his personal space. I inhaled and took in a subtle combination of shampoo, deodorant and laundry detergent. The scent of a man has always been important to me. When I took his in, a slight flutter in my stomach caused me to pull away a little too quickly. He turned to his truck and graciously opened the door for me. I thanked him and climbed into the seat, then nervously smiled as he made sure I was comfortably in and gently shut the door for me as well. I don't think a man had ever done that for me before in my life. I forced myself to remember that he had been late.

The thing about him was that he broke the three-day rule. I gave him my number after we were introduced by a mutual friend at a bar one night. I had quit drinking alcohol and was rarely seen socializing in a bar for more than forty-five minutes. But that night, I found myself downing Red Bull after Red Bull and chain-smoking my American Spirits, just so I could chat with him a little bit longer. We hit it off by talking about music—our favorite bands, favorite albums, favorite songs. He was a musician. A singer-songwriter who played guitar. I had always told myself that I would marry a musician—if I ever got married. And as much as I wanted to go home and crawl into bed, I just couldn't pull my attention away from him. I wanted him to take me home that night, but I didn't want to be that type of girl anymore. So when he asked for my number, I gave it to him. And he called two days later. He had found out that one of the bands we both liked was playing a show the following night. I imagined that he must have gone home and done some thorough internet research to find an enticing reason to ask me out. He had done a good job because I didn't have to think twice to say "yes."

We drove to a cute little Brazilian restaurant in Silverlake. I had passed it many times but had never set foot inside before. As the valet helped me out of the truck, he ran ahead to hold the door to the restaurant open for me. We took a seat by the window and I immediately switched my focus to the menu. He made some recommendations and we decided to go family style. We conversed about the simple things first—how long we had been in L.A., what we came here for, what we were doing with our time these days. When I asked him what he did for work he looked down at his hands and blushed.

"Well, I'm unemployed right now," he stammered.

Oh great, I thought. My ex-boyfriend was unemployed for the entire few months we had been together, and not only had it made him extremely moody when the slightest talk of money was brought up, it also prevented him from getting out of bed on a daily basis. Strike two.

"I worked for an independent record label for five years," he continued. "It was a great job and I really enjoyed it, but then I got promoted to management and I was stuck behind a desk for the last couple of years. And I thought, 'What am I doing? This isn't what I want,' so I quit that job. Then I had my own eBay business for a while. But I'm in a production of Romeo & Juliet right now with a company that tours public schools, and that pays. But we haven't rehearsed or had a show in a couple months, so, unfortunately, I haven't gotten a paycheck from them in a while."

Strike three. I had dated an actor once. And it wasn't a problem then, but I had just always thought actors were obnoxious and egotistical. I mean, I'm an actor, and I know I'm obnoxious and egotistical. I was just never really enticed by the idea of dating someone who was in the same professional field as me. And I was especially turned-off by actor-musicians. I just always thought that either art form is extremely demanding and difficult, and if a person splits his commitment between the two, he could never be truly dedicated and succeed in one. Of course, a lot of the things that I used to think have recently been revealed to me as complete bullshit. But for whatever reason, when I learned that he seemed to be more focused on his acting than his music, I was undoubtedly disappointed.

"Oh, that's cool," I forced a smile.

Throughout the meal, I was continuously caught off-guard because every time he told me something about himself, he would turn the conversation back over to me and urge me to tell him something about myself. In my experience, that was extremely rare. Normally if I was sitting down with a man, or just on the phone with him, he would just talk and talk and talk and I would throw in an occasional "Mm hmm" or "Okay." So that night I wasn't prepared to reveal so much about myself. I chose my words wisely because I had no intention of pursuing any sort of relationship with this man. And I found no reason to share too much about myself with someone I probably wouldn't see again. But when I did speak, he looked me directly in the eyes, and didn't flinch until I was completely finished. Then he would take a bite of food and respond to what I had just said or ask me about something else. And again, when I spoke, he kept his focus entirely on me, then repeated the process. Occasionally, when he was speaking, I'd find myself thoroughly evaluating his features and mannerisms. I could still hear and comprehend what he was saying, but his voice would start to sound hollow, as if I were under water and he was just above the surface. He really was an extraordinarily attractive being. The shape of his face was beautifully defined—a distinct chin and sharp cheekbones that ensured he was a fully developed man but maintained an aura of youth around him. His eyes were dark but not threatening, his lips were soft but not feminine. His hair was well-kept, but not too well-kept. There wasn't a single blemish, scar or mark on his skin. I suddenly became extremely self-conscious. Physically, he was the type of man who made my heart skip a beat when he looked at me, but would fuck me once then disappear. I couldn't comprehend why he would want to be seen in public with a girl like me.

"Shall we get going?" His voice came back to me at full volume. I smiled and nodded.

The show we were going to see was up at Universal, which is never a stress-free place to go. I could sense that he was getting frustrated as we circled the parking lot a third time. I almost felt embarrassed for him because I could tell he was determined to make the night flawless, and sometimes even a little thing like parking can become such an unnecessary inconvenience. But we made it and began the trek toward the amphitheatre. It was a beautiful evening—not too cold or windy. As we walked, he always stayed right beside me—never ahead and never behind. Occasionally we'd bump shoulders, which was followed by an awkward apology. Once we were inside I could hear the muted echo of the band already playing. Normally, I would have been annoyed. I absolutely hate being late and usually try to blame someone other than myself for my tardiness. But for some reason, it didn't bother me at all that night. For the first time in years, I truly felt at ease in the presence of another person. We rushed to find our seats, which were supposedly on the mezzanine level. We quickly learned that the mezzanine level meant the nose-bleed section.

"Wow, we're really far away," he commented. "Should have brought my binoculars."

"Well, at least we can make-out up here," I teased.

He laughed. Nervously. Maybe it was a little too soon for me to be making lame jokes. It's usually just a cover for being uncomfortable.

He used the display light from his cell phone to find our seats in the dark. We were really far away. Almost to the point where it no longer seems like the music is live, which is one of the main reasons I don't particularly like large venues. But the benefit of being in seats rather than in the pit that night was that I didn't have to worry about making an ass out of myself by dancing or jumping around. We settled down as quickly as possible so as not to miss anymore of the band's set list. Every once in a while he'd lean in to make a quick comment in my ear or vice versa, but for the most part, we both just focused on the music. I could sense the energy of his presence next to me, which was comforting, but it was pleasant to not feel obligated to constantly turn and acknowledge him. At one point, the band began playing a song that I wasn't familiar with. It was off their newest album, which I hadn't gotten around to affording yet. But from the moment it started, I knew that it was going to be my favorite song of the night. I could feel the reverb bounce off the walls and vibrate inside my chest. It was as if a sudden rush of adrenaline soared through my body. But I didn't have to waste it on anything so I was able to experience the euphoria of a natural high. And for a moment, the building, the thousands of screaming fans, even the band on stage—they just disappeared, and it was just me and him and this song. And it was beautiful.

When it was over, I turned to him and said, "I really liked that one."

"It's off their new album."

"Yeah, I think I remember hearing it in the car."

We were both slightly disappointed in having missed most of the set, so we agreed to stay and check out the headlining artist. She had an amazing voice and I recognized one song from my last radio phase, but the style was very mellow and I soon felt my eyelids growing heavy. I took this sudden moment of solemn relaxation as an opportunity to lean my head on his shoulder. He promptly settled his arm around me and I allowed myself to melt into the familiar warmth of a man.

"You getting sleepy?" he murmured.

"Mmm."

We stayed for a couple more songs, sinking further and further into our seats, before we snuck out. It was nice to leave early, when no one else was around as we made the long trek back from the amphitheater to the parking lot. We remained interlocked in each other's arms as we made small talk, commenting on everything from the music to the neon signs lighting each store front we passed. And I felt unusually comfortable.

Again, when we reached his truck, he opened the door for me and watched me clumsily climb in. Looking back, I have to wonder if that is simply a tactic men use to check out a woman's ass and earn brownie points at the same time. Regardless, I struggled my way into the seat, pausing briefly on the way up to place my purse on the floor, arch my back ever-so-slightly, and give him the best view I could offer. I assumed I had left him with some sort of visual fantasy at the least based on the moment of silence we sat in together once he had situated himself in the driver's seat.

"So..." he finally started, "What should we do now?"

"Oh, I don't care," I replied, which was a lie since my preference would have been for him to take me home and do whatever he pleased with me. But if the date were to result as a one-night stand and I were to never see him again, I didn't want to be the one who instigated it. I had decided that I'd rather not get any than to get it only once. And I had told myself that I wasn't going to put out so easy anymore.

"Um, I'm not sure what's still open around here other than bars and clubs," he continued. "There's always bowling or we could shoot some pool."

"That sounds fun," I attempted to sound convincing. "But I think I feel like doing something by ourselves. Or at least going somewhere quiet. That music made me all, like, relaxed."

"Yeah, I'd prefer that too."

"Do you like to go night-driving?"

"What? You mean, just driving around?"

"Well, yeah. At night. With the windows down. Just drive for a little bit, not going anywhere in particular."

"Yeah. I used to do that all the time when gas wasn't so expensive."

"Me too. Maybe we could do that."

I was surprised when he enthusiastically agreed. I don't think night-driving is something one would normally propose on a first date. At least not without the huge risk of coming off as completely lame.

"There's this road off Mulholland that I used to take a lot," he suggested. "It's got a beautiful view."

"Let's do it."

Without missing a beat, he started the engine and led us out on our journey. It wasn't too late yet, maybe ten-o-clock, but it was a Monday night, so the freeway was pretty wide open. As we traveled progressively further away from the city and closer to the dry mountains, the landscape around us grew dimmer and eventually became a mere silhouette. When I turned to look at him, I could no longer make out the shades or depth of his face. Occasionally the reflection of some light bounced off the moisture of his eyes, informing me that he was looking in my direction. Overall I felt pretty masked—present, but somewhat hidden in the illusion of privacy. Soon we exited the freeway and the illumination of a flashing red signal light suddenly made me aware that I was tensely massaging the inside of my thigh.

Soon the road got thinner and the curves came more often. We drove mostly in silence, broken only on occasion with small talk to ensure that the other person didn't feel bored or boring. I lifted the compartment in his truck that separated the two of us in order to slide closer to him. I felt him tense slightly as I wrapped my arm around his neck and pulled myself close enough to whisper into his ear.

"Thanks for taking me out tonight." I intentionally made sure that my lower lip just barely brushed the top of his ear lobe as I spoke.

"You're welcome." He turned to me, just long enough to make eye contact, then focused back on the dark road. "We're almost there," he added.

I nuzzled my nose into his neck, minimizing the space between our bodies as much as I thought appropriate. Then I slid my hand from his knee and up his thigh. He immediately flinched and released a sort of high-pitched squeal without completely losing his manhood, which caused me to burst into laughter.

"That tickled," he defended himself.

I sat back in my seat and kept my eyes forward as we eventually slowed to a stop. We were surrounded by a thin fog that added an ethereal element to the dark mountainside. We stepped out of his truck, but stayed close by to keep watch for police cars patrolling the illegal parking zone. He retrieved a large windbreaker from behind his seat and spread it out on the dirt for us to sit on. The view was quite spectacular for Los Angeles' standards. Everything east of the mountain was visible, but only in the form of colorful lights and vague silhouettes. A low hum from the freeway below was barely audible. For a moment, I felt like we were the only two people left on the planet, and I was completely okay with that.

There was a slight sting to the cold breeze, so he wrapped his arms around me tightly. Against his body, I felt warm and safe and beautiful. We caught eyes and stared at each other for what seemed like an eternity. But it wasn't awkward or uncomfortable. It was as if we were trying to see inside one another, to figure the other person out. And then he kissed me. He moved in slowly, to make sure that I approved. When our lips touched, the cold melted away and a warm, tingling sensation swam through my body. It felt like a sip of hot cocoa moving down my throat and into my stomach while sitting by the fireside on a snowy winter evening. But better.

When I opened my mouth, he brushed his tongue against mine. It felt soft, like velvet. Every move he made I responded to. No matter where or how we touched, our pores linked together like perfectly fitted puzzle pieces. Something about his kiss was different from anything I had ever experienced before in my life. I couldn't decipher what it was. He felt so indescribably good, but not in a purely sexual way. In a way that I believed must be one of the truly beautiful things in human existence. In a way that felt like a reason to live.

As I drifted into a state of euphoria, his hands slipped under my shirt and began to massage my back. His skin felt soft and comforting. I followed his lead and slid my fingers across his stomach. I played with the thin line of fuzz trailing from the center of his ribs down to his belt. I wanted to follow it further, but hesitated about moving too fast. Instead, I snuck my index finger under the waist of his pants to explore just a couple more inches. He adjusted his body until his pelvis was closer to me. He opened himself up in a way that communicated that my touch was welcome. So I placed my other hand on his knee, then slowly moved upward and squeezed his inner thigh. This time it didn't tickle. Instead, I felt the vibration of a low moan escape his throat and bounce against my lips. So I continue moving my hand until it was cupped around his crotch. Through his clothing, I could feel that he had started to become erect. I explored the shape of his cock and rubbed against it. He attempted to squeeze his hands down the back of my jeans. But the tightness of my pants didn't allow him to reach my ass. So I quickly unbuttoned and unzipped them to allow him more room. Then I returned my hand to his hardness. He hungrily grabbed my ass, rubbing his palms against it then massaging it. When I moved to undo his belt and unzip his pants, he didn't stop me. Instead, he kissed me harder. I grabbed him again, beneath his pants, but over his underwear. His cock felt large and perfectly constructed. Everything about him felt so good that I thought I was high. But a far better high than any drug or substance could produce. I yearned for him to be inside of me. But I worried about him becoming a one-night stand. I wanted him for more than just one night.

Despite my fears, I chose to act compulsively. I pulled away from him and leaned backwards until I was laying flat on the ground with only the windbreaker serving as a blanket. I slid out of my jeans completely and kicked them aside onto the dirt. This time, he followed my lead. He pulled down his pants but left them hanging around his ankles. Somewhat paranoid, he glanced around, making sure that no one else was around and that no cars were approaching. Then he fell on top of me. Our mouths linked again and nothing could stop us. Hiding me with his own body, he pulled my panties off just enough for him to rub his hand against my vagina. I hadn't realized how wet I already was until I felt his hand become thoroughly lubricated when he touched me. He slipped his finger inside of me and, again, a warm, comforting sensation flowed through my body. Although his touch was new to me, it felt like it had always belonged.

"Is this okay?" he whispered.

I nodded, although I was unsure of exactly what he was referring to. But then I felt his bare, erect cock gently pressed against my inner thigh and I realized he had removed his underwear as well. At first he rubbed against me, gyrating his hips so the length of his penis moved up and down my clit until it too became lubricated by my wetness. As he maintained a consistent repetition, I timed his movement so I knew exactly when he was beginning his descent backwards. Then I lifted my hips and arched my back just slightly, so when he pushed forward again, he glided straight inside of me. The moment he entered, we both simultaneously released a long, soft moan. He fit perfectly and felt better than any man I had ever been with before. With our bodies linked together, I was convinced he was a limb that had been amputated from me so long ago and had suddenly reappeared. We fell into a rhythm as if we had done this many times before. But the sensations shooting through my body reminded me that we never had. I wrapped my legs around him, my ankles linked together. And each time he retracted, I flexed every muscle in my vagina to tighten its grasp around him. Even in the brisk night air, I could see tiny beads of sweat forming around his face and on his neck. Under the dim glow of the distant city lights, he glistened like a diamond.

It wasn't too long before he came. Mainly, I thought, because he was worried that a car would soon pass by, even though none had since our arrival. He squinted his eyes and scrunched up his nose. He dropped his jaw until his mouth was stretched wide open, but no sound came out, as if he were screaming from the other side of a sound proof window. Then at the very last moment, he raced to pull out of me. His cum shot in several long streaks and landed in the dirt beside us. As soon as he was drained, he collapsed on top of me. I wrapped my arms around him again, my hands clutching his back where his shirt had grown moist with sweat. He kissed me, pressing his lips against mine and simply holding them there. We laid still for a moment, silent, as if we were one being.

"Let's get back in the truck," he mumbled, our lips still attached.

"Okay."

He struggled to pick himself back up and redress. I remained on my back as I pulled up my jeans and underwear, and suddenly felt the consequences of lying on the hard, uneven ground. We glanced around, making sure we had everything, and hurried into his truck. He started the engine and blasted the heat. I laid my head in his lap, curled up like a kitten, as we drove to my apartment. We cuddled together in my bed, talking, then making love again, then talking some more. I told him some of the worst things about myself and my past—things no sane person would ever share on a first date. But I was determined to get everything out in the open from the get-go. I didn't want to risk growing attached to someone who would be frightened away after he'd really gotten to know me. I suppose a part of me was actually trying to scare him off. I knew that it would hurt less for him to leave me now than leave me later. But he stayed. When I woke the next morning, he was still naked in my bed. And he looked even more beautiful than I remembered from the night before.

And just like that, I fell in love. He knows all of my secrets and he's still here. We still make love as if nothing else in the world mattered. We still cuddle and talk, except now we discuss marriage and the names of our children. We argue then apologize. We carry each other when we can't walk alone. We cook meals for one another and drink coffee together in the mornings. We do crossword puzzles in bed. And I've realized that I don't need anyone else. I don't want anyone else ever again. I want to grow up with him, grow old with him, pass away with him. Despite my defiance in the beginning, I've fallen in love. And I've fallen hard. But I haven't hit the ground yet and I hope I never do.

He is my last story.